Margo Glantz

The Wake

Translated from the Spanish
by Andrew Hurley

CURBSTONE PRESS

A Lannan Translation Selection
with Special Thanks to Patrick Lannan and
the Lannan Foundation Board of Directors

Printed in the U.S. on acid-free paper by BookMobile
Cover design by Shapiro Design
Cover artwork:"Woman at the Piano," Philip Evergood, 1955, oil
on canvas; by permission of the Smithsonian American Art
Museum, DC/Art Resource, NY.

This book was published with the support
of the Connecticut Commission on Culture
and Tourism, Lannan Foundation, National
NATIONAL ENDOWMENT FOR THE ARTS Endowment for the Arts, and donations
from many individuals. We are very
grateful for this support.

Connecticut Commission on Culture & Tourism

Library of Congress Cataloging-in-Publication Data

Glantz, Margo.
  [Rastro. English]
  The wake / Marco Glantz ; translated from the Spanish by
Andrew Hurley.— 1st ed.
      p. cm.
  ISBN 1-931896-23-2 (pbk. : alk. paper)
  I. Hurley, Andrew. II. Title.
  PQ7298.17.L36R3713 2005
  863'.64—dc22   2005014462
  ISBN-13: 978-1-931896-23-8

published by
CURBSTONE PRESS   321 Jackson St. Willimantic, CT 06226
      phone: 860-423-5110   e-mail: info@curbstone.org
                  http://www.curbstone.org

For Ariel

A-dying, a-dying we all go. . .

PEDRO CALDERÓN DE LA BARCA

Esta tarde, mi bien, cuando te hablaba,
como en tu rostro y tus acciones vía
que con palabras no te persuadía,
que el corazón me vieses deseaba;

y Amor, que mis intentos ayudaba,
venció lo que imposible parecía:
pues entre el llanto, que el dolor vertía,
el corazón deshecho destilaba.

baste ya de rigores, mi bien, baste:
no te atormenten más celos tiranos,
ni el vil recelo tu quietud contraste

con sombras necias, con indicios vanos,
pues ya en líquido humor viste y tocaste
mi corazón deshecho entre tus manos.

SOR JUANA INÉS DE LA CRUZ

This evening, my darling, when we spoke,
As in thy face and in thy actions I could see
That my words in persuading thee were vain,
I wished thou might'st but see one time into my heart;

And Love, who to my entreaties did harken,
Gained what else impossible to gain had been,
For into tears, which mine eyes poured forth,
My broken heart its message full distilled.

Enough cold-heartedness, my darling, enough!
Be wracked no more by tyrant jealousy,
Nor let vile suspicion stir thy calm temperament

With silly shadows, dire yet foolish omens,
For thou hast seen and touched in liquid humor
My heart shattered in thy hands.

Castration has a second purpose: it allows the natural scale of voices to be altered. It frees the human voice from dependence upon sex and dependence upon age.

PASCAL QUIGNARD

If I can take a breather, the pain is over.

musical group "MONO BLANCO"

Lastima, bandoneón,
mi corazón,
tu ronca maldición maleva...
Tu lágrima de ron me lleva
hasta el hondo bajo fondo
donde el barro se subleva.
Ya sé, no me digás. ¡Tenés razón!
La vida es una herida absurda,
y es todo, todo, tan fugaz,
que es una curda, ¡nada más!
mi confesión...

LA ÚLTIMA CURDA (tango)[1]

Damn you, bandoneón,[2]
your heartless boozy curse
has dealt my heart a mortal wound...
And your tears of rum
are carrying me down
into the deep dark hole
where the clay revolts.
I know—don't tell me! I know!
Life is an absurd wound,
and it is all, all, so fleeting,
so what to do but drink myself to death—
I must confess...

THE LAST BINGE

[1] Music by Aníbal Troilo, lyrics by Cátulo Castillo (1956).
[2] The accordion-like instrument typically used to play the tango.

My name is Nora García.

I haven't been back to this town for years: I park my car, approach the front door timidly, cautiously, and step inside. I hardly recognize the house; it's fallen on hard times, the lawn unattended, the plants dry, the grass sparse and yellow, some places where there had once been flowering shrubs now bare, barren. Down below, in the gully, trees with broad limbs and green leaves and brightly-colored flowers. People everywhere; I feel shy, tentative, my heart shrinks inside me: I know several people, not exactly the ones I was closest to, others that I've forgotten, perhaps—it's been a long time. I think I recognize one woman, but her body is swollen, her face swollen, her color is not good—might this be a funereal color? I'm exaggerating, I tell myself, it's the news of his death, the return to this house, the fear of remembering too much, the conviction that I'll be seeing people I hate, people who have hurt me—the usual, I tell myself, the uncertainties of the heart. The woman's name escapes me. She's looking at me—mockingly? contemptuously? or is it just a greeting? Maybe that's the way people look at one another at funerals, maybe that's just life, as my mother would always say—my mother, rest her soul, as Juan's soul is resting now, or so I hope—may he truly rest in peace.

I nod, silently, to the people helping in the house, and then I make my way into the living room, where the body is laid out—it's a large room, enormous actually, full of musical instruments, with scores scattered on a long table beside the computers and still-virgin music paper ruled with staves (: scores? there are still scores?).

I look around, along the walls of bookshelves filled with books, the way it should be, books in bookshelves, the pictures on the walls, the water stains.

1

Several people standing before the casket.

I approach.

Like so many coffins, this one has a kind of window—could it be a door?—that lets you see part of the body. His face is livid, I suppose that's only natural, it's simple enough, he's dead, the faces of dead people have no color, their heart has stopped beating, that's right, I tell myself, that's right, he's dead. He's dead, he's not breathing anymore, his heart has stopped beating, his blood has stopped circulating. I snoop around a bit, then stop moving, stand attentive, suspended, I'm curious to know what it is I feel, but the truth is, I don't feel anything, anything; my pulse is calm, rhythmic, normal: a hundred beats a minute. There is a strong smell of mold, of mildew, it's everywhere—in the room, on the coffin, on my body, now I smell of mildew, of mustiness, of dense humidity. Someone steps away from the casket, I approach to see better, see him better, see Juan better. I lean over, almost touch his face with my cheek; his hands are crossed over his chest, and he is holding a cross: I didn't expect that. What a strange color his face is, olive, a kind of yellow! As though he were dead, I think, oh but that's right, it's only natural, that's the way it is, yes, of course, it's just that simple: he's dead, his heart has stopped beating. A small gray, or ash-colored, moustache covers his lips, now thinner than before, his skin is transparent, his cheeks are bony, protuberant, his high forehead, like an open carrying-case, frames his eyes, which are sunken, and his eyelids are profoundly closed. The casket, white pine with fittings of gold-colored metal; leaning against the walls, several wreaths: they cover the pictures. On the bookshelves there are wreaths, too: they cover the books. Candles around the coffin, four of them. And the sickly-sweet smell, the smell of mold (why does that surprise me? it's hot and wet here), the dense smell of mildew. Juan is wearing a sport coat the color of dry hay that goes with the yellowness of his face and the color of the wood. His shirt and tie are the same color. This is a makeshift chapel, full of people, books, pictures, musical instruments, a long grand piano with the top up, a Bösendorfer with a score on the music stand, and beside it the harpsichord, its top open too, beautifully decorated with baroque motifs, a delicate landscape drawn very softly, almost idyllically in tones of pastel. (Where's the Steinway? I don't see it.) Off in a corner, dressed in black, a downcast-looking figure. Standing beside me, a smooth-skinned, beardless man wearing rough cotton pants and a straw hat, as though to protect himself from the sun where there's no sun. A dog comes in, a female dog, a bitch, very skinny, bones showing through her skin, with yellow teeth, a long narrow muzzle, black teats hanging down to the floor—she's just given birth and looks hungry; no one throws her out of the room; she approaches the coffin, brushes me with her tail, (snoops around a bit) (like I did), then puts out her front paws and stretches, her black teats— so many of them!—spreading out on the floor. I lean over the coffin again, to see him better, to observe him, to capture the tiniest details of his death (of his corporeal death), and what I find is an unfamiliar crucifix between his arms and a sparse, leaden moustache—hard or stiff?, prickly?, waxed?, a moustache that totally changes his face, disguises it, degrades it.

A woman offers me a drink (Herradura Reposada), and I accept with my heart in my throat (a short, very well dressed, ceremonious man comes in, approaches the coffin and in a pompous voice, a pompous diction out of proportion to his stature, asks the woman serving the tequila: Are you the bereaved to whom I should offer my most heartfelt condolences? Shaking her head, the woman moves, quickly, toward the front door.) (Shouldn't he have asked me? Am I not the one to whom he should be offering his condolences?) (I, Nora García?) There is nothing, will be nothing to remove me from this sickly-sweet smell of mildew or clotted blood. It nauseates me. I leave the room, bump into someone that says hello. I don't answer, I walk toward the back yard, try not to look at anyone: the smell surrounds me, follows me, dogs my steps, densely. It's hot here, very hot, and I am not dressed for this—I'm wearing a sweater, pants, and boots. Fortunately, I've just cut my hair, and that makes me look younger. I pretend not to know the people that used to upset me so much when I was with Juan, when the children were still children and the cat and dogs lived harmoniously together, despite the old saying, because they would never fight like cats and dogs, they would play, play almost as though they were the same species, breed, and sex, the female sometimes mounting the male, the male sometimes mounting the female, they would jump, pant, throw themselves on top of each other, the cats and the dogs or just the dogs, I mean the cat, singular, with the dogs, because there was only one cat and a lot of dogs; the dogs rolling around with each other, playing with innocent furor (it's a very big yard) (there are many plants, many trees on the lower part of the property), the dogs would growl, howl, bark, lick, nip at each other or show their teeth, wind their tails around each other, white or yellow, chocolate-colored or black, with lots of hair or little, and a rank smell of cat was everywhere, the smell of tomcat on the prowl for females.

Out in the yard, tall men and short, some very elegant, others dressed casually or very humbly, one with his head shaved, the entire dome covered with tattoos, heavyset women like the one I described before and am now looking for but who is no longer anywhere to be found; instead, a young woman with dark fuzz above her upper lip; many of these people (mourners?) with only fair (or even devastated) complexions, brown-skinned, black-skinned, tan, fair-skinned, blue eyes, black eyes, dark hair, many with moustaches, others smooth-skinned, some dressed humbly, others far too elegantly for a house in the country, but all, without exception, including the man with the tattoos (how strange! do you suppose it hurt much to have himself covered with those inscriptions that begin on his forehead and run

back over his head down to the nape of his neck?), are holding
a glass and talking, laughing, winking. One group especially,
several men in very well-cut cashmere suits, their postures
uncomfortable: a rigidity that matches their moustaches—
almost all of the moustaches bushy, although in different cuts
and shapes (only one of the men has a beard), yes, I am struck
by the abundance of moustaches: prickly, rigid, bushy, wild
or well-groomed, little, long, curly, blond, black. One man
with a black moustache, under it a timid little smile. Another,
his goatee very sparse, not very neat, over there a fair-skinned
man with a blond moustache, very long, the ends twirled up
till they almost reach his eyes, and he's twirling one tip with
his fingers. The moustache on the tall, handsome man with
fair skin is very thick, dark, silky, broad and well-trimmed,
and he has a wide smile, like a rabbit. Juan has also let his
moustache grow—stiff, and prickly. I watch them out of the
corner of my eye—standing solemn, stiff, although they've
drunk a great deal, their bodies maintaining the rigidity of a
musical instrument, a cello, for example, and when someone
comes over to greet them, the affectionate, ritual back-
slappings are loud in the air, a counterpoint to the sound of
the guitars, quavering trumpets, and out-of-tune violins of
the mariachis, the mariachis that won't stop singing (the
wrinkled, emaciated face, the quivering flesh) (when they
sing, their moustaches quiver), dressed in their brownish-gray
charro suits, the fake-silver studs, the faded patriotic colors
of their ties, the double row of buttons down their pants,
accentuating their bow-legs. In another group there are two
women, dressed very much alike, almost replicas of one
another, one light-skinned, the other dark, one tall, the other
thin and small, one's eyes clear, serene, the other's with a
reddish glint, or reflection, their clothes almost identical, one
in a long skirt and high-heeled sandals, the other in pants
and flats, but both in white, as though they were on vacation
at a fancy beach resort...white clothes at a funeral?, I ask
myself: Why not? One of the women is wearing a lot of silver

necklaces; the little one is wearing diamond rings and gold necklaces. A fashion show, the society page of the newspaper. A man in front of me, with an absent, self-absorbed expression, lays his hand on his crotch; he is tall, dark, with light hair, green eyes, he opens his mouth and I see two gold canines. Beside him, the mariachis are still singing—the mariachis had been singing—and the buttons on their suits are made of some cheap metal, now rusty. One of the mourners, dressed very formally, very ceremoniously, goes over to the mariachis and starts singing (with emphasis and ardor) a song by José Alfredo Jiménez, as though it were an aria from an opera: the harsh clang of a string snapping; he plants his feet firmly (they are tiny) to sing better, and his moustache quivers. Several campesinos nearby, gaunt, with emaciated faces, wearing palm-leaf hats, white shirts, canvas trousers, others dressed in the old indigenous dress, with trousers of thick, rough cotton. A dwarf—is he not a flautist? Waiters with trays of little sandwiches and glasses of tequila circulate constantly (why is there no wine? isn't red wine supposed to make good strong blood?), and in the kitchen the servants are preparing a meal. A strong smell of smoking-hot oil infects the air.

Among the guests, those whose trade is making music are the great majority—pianists, singers, sopranos, contraltos, basses, baritones, countertenors, conductors, cellists (I, too, am a cellist), violinists and violists, oboists, saxophonists, composers, scholars and academics, a male flautist (who plays the recorder), a female flautist (who plays the silver flute), a percussionist, the critic who writes for the cultural supplements. What did I expect? How could it be any other way? What's so strange about seeing a famous flautist, a percussionist, an opera singer, in the house of a composer, conductor, and great pianist who has just died?

Wept over more because this is a funeral than because he is dead?

Is the enormous living room—where he is laid out—not

filled with musical instruments, old scores, records, music books, biographies of composers? Scores? yes, scores too. Recordings and scores by Bach, Schubert, Pergolesi, Haydn, Monteverdi, Händel, Schumann, Beethoven, Vivaldi, Campra; recordings by pianists, only pianists: Glenn Gould, Horowitz, Rubinstein, Wilhelm Kempff, Walter Gieseking, Arturo Benedetti Michelangelo, Sviatoslav Richter, Claudio Arrau, Marta Argerich, András Schiff, Emil Gilels, Vladimir Ashkenazy, Maria João Pires, Radu Lupu. Records, too, wax, and the kind of record players people used to use; many CDs, and DVDs, memorable performances of nineteenth-century operas by Callas, René Jacobs, Kathleen Battle, Teresa Stratas, Andreas Scholl, Cecilia Bartoli, Pavarotti, Plácido Domingo; a recording of the last castrati with their shrieking voices, shrieking like a cat being castrated. I remember the performances, I can almost hear them (the old ones, still on heavy 78-RPM records: Caruso, Tebaldi, Vickers, Chaliapin, Schwarzkopf), I can almost hear the performers, see them as they eternally sing their arias, gesticulating, majestic, declamatory, their mouths open wide, their arms raised high, appearing in Aida and La Traviata, in L'Orphée (et Euridice), Dido and Aeneas, Ulysses (the return of), and Xerxes (by Händel) (now so fashionable), sung by David Daniels, a countertenor (in Spanish, contratenor; in French, haut-contre).

I go back to the house and into the living room where he is laid out: the air is humid, sticky. On the piano, two glasses, half-drunk, one with traces of dark lipstick. I find a place for myself beside the coffin, lean over, look fixedly at Juan, observe him with morbid interest, review the details of his face, his clothing, the coffin; I enumerate them, and, very softly, as though I were praying, I tune some of my impressions, then begin to hum them, accompany those praying the rosary, as though that murmur helped to mute the dense smell of mildew. How strange! I say to myself again, they've put a cross in his hands, it's lying there on his chest. How beautiful his hands were! The chest, that shell of bones and muscles that protects the heart! (The heart is simply a muscle, a pump that pushes liquid through our bodies, an extraordinary machine.) (I smell cigarette smoke.) The color of his face is sepulchral. What color did I expect his face to be? I am intrigued by his moustache, very fine, very gray, sparse, ash-colored actually, prickly—waxed? He'd never worn a moustache before; it looks like a caricature, a parody, a moustache that doesn't quite make it to gray—the color of burned hay (like the enormous bales in staggering lines down the fields when I'm driving to this town, the bales the same color as his corduroy jacket), the coffin of white pine with fittings of embossed gold metal, the wreaths leaning against the walls, giving off their heavy fragrance. Still, neither the fragrance of the flowers nor the smell of the burning wax mitigates the sickly-sweet smell that surrounds the body like an aureola—it spreads, envelops me, begins to suffocate me, gives me anxiety. I lean over his face again, observe it, look at it, look at his face, his body—what I can see of his body—, review and repeat the details, one by one: the banal tie he's wearing, the green-hay-colored jacket, the coffin of rough light-colored wood, its vulgarity. Juan, yes, Juan, who loved well-cut clothes, good ties (designer ties), impeccable shirts (made to order, always in good taste), cashmere sweaters, Armani suits, Balenciaga ties. What a shame!, I can't see his shoes. I wonder what color they are. And what about his socks? (Am I turning stupid?) I raise my eyes and look at his face again. How could I possibly not have noticed before? A black kerchief holds his jaw closed, intensifies the lividity of his face, which is set off by the burned-hay color of his suit and matches the color of the wood, but not the sickly-sweet smell of clotted blood that surrounds me, envelops me, encircles me, as though it were an aureola.

I close my eyes: I see him now, lying there before me, almost naked, on a table, needles sticking out of his body—

his chest, his belly, his ears, above his eyelashes, his forehead sad-looking from thinking about life—and in the skin of his neck, near the jugular, a tense needle. I'm so tired I can't sleep, and every time I dream about him, it's another life I've lived. I keep standing there, before the body; his eyes are closed, a needle stuck in him near his navel, his smooth skin. A slightly reddish color traces the needle's path; on his belly and across his chest, around his nipples, silky black hair, the pink aureolas, the almost nonexistent nipples. With my eyes always closed, every time I dream about him, it's another life I'm living, the needles stuck into the middle of his forehead, my forehead, the forehead of the death that's come to close his eyes, my eyes that died when they saw him, saw him like that, with two needles, diagonal, as though suspended in air, vibrating on the bone. I extend my hands, put my right hand on his left leg, he shivers, lifts it, flexes it. I run my hand along it slowly, touch his knee, lean over him and lay my palm on his warm chest: life is an absurd wound, it has transfixed my heart. His heart is calm (50 to 100 beats a minute), the blanket covering him opens a bit and a fragment of his left thigh is exposed, I shudder, and shudder again as I did when we were young: 100 beats per minute or more?, tachycardia?, yes, one's pulse—my pulse—accelerates: the heart is just a muscle, a pump that pumps liquid through our body and keeps it alive (the heart sends venous blood to the lungs, and when the blood is oxygenated it returns as arterial blood and is immediately distributed throughout the organism). My heart: I wear my heart on my eyes, as the poem says.

I open my eyes and there he is again, immobile, I am absorbed by the image of death by needles, the window in the coffin reveals his face, his livid color, that gray, out of place, stiff, useless moustache, the black kerchief holding his lower jaw tight, the moss-green jacket, the banal tie (under his clothes, his heart has stopped beating) and the smell, always the smell, the dense and suffocating smell of mold, of mildew.

I am uncomfortable everywhere. I go outside again, my movements jerky, convulsive, walk out into the yard. There are groups here and there, near the hedges, on the slopes, on the edge of the gully. People are walking on the grass, throwing cigarettes (some lighted) into the rosebushes; nearby, bougainvillea growing over the walls, its color as bright as the metallic register of trumpets. Snippets of conversations here and there (I dreamed that I got lost), random words (: I woke up furious), scattered words (: I was looking everywhere for myself, but I couldn't find me.), hypocritical sentences: they're hurtful, some of them leave wounds (To whom should I offer my most heartfelt condolences?, someone says, in an attack of statesmanly rhetoric), create a language that, though mutilated, inscribes itself on one's skin like a tattoo. Tattoo: it covers his flesh, the air, it masks the pain, the tattoo of the needles that pierce his skin, a shield, a mask, Medusa. The only thing true, the only thing real, is that which does not exist. The heart has impulses that reason knows nothing about. An insensitive person, incapable of being moved by the pain of others, has a heart of stone. Ezequiel foretells it in the Old Testament: In hearts turned to stone, God performs a spiritual transplant. The sick man who received an artificial heart has just died of a metal myocardial infarction, a failure of his metal heart.

I see, hear a man in the yard, surrounded by people, talking in a very loud, pompous (fatuous) voice. The difficulty stems from the easiness, it's just that simple, I tell you, just that simple to die, a person dies when his heart stops—you have failed me, oh my heart—that's it, it's just that simple. He's an old friend of Juan's (and once, of mine), and he gives me an imperceptible wink of recognition and repeats: the difficulty stems from the easiness, it's simple, his heart just blew. He is huge, bearded, and old, and in one of his hands—immense, wrinkled, greasy, hairy, voluminous—he is holding a glass of tequila (King Kong climbs the Empire State Building carrying the blond damsel), his drooping eyelids give him a sleepy look, despite the fact that his eyes are enormous and very wide open. A broad nose, a large mouth despite its thinness, long thin lips, lines at the side of his mouth matching his droopy eyes: he is not wearing a moustache. When he speaks, his lips tighten into a voracious, contemptuous grimace. A pale, thin, small woman, perfectly coiffed, perfectly dressed, without makeup, without a single piece of jewelry, ascetic (viperous?) (her heart sullied by the world's contagion?), stands beside Eduardo, making him gigantic: she smiles mechanically. The others look at him as though enraptured: in the banality of his discourse, several intentions mingle. The sound of a voice behind him, a tanned, weather-beaten man, with a sweet, timid moustache: Do you really think death warns us? It just comes like *that*, all of a sudden, when we least expect it. Silence falls again, I walk away. It's true, I think, it doesn't warn us, it just comes, like *that*, without speaking to us once. I am not interested in how easy it is to reach perfection, even if that easiness should imply that his heart has blown, his heart has shattered (mine has been broken too), yes, life, the absurd wound that is life, yes, it's true, the heart is simply a muscle that pumps liquid through our bodies and keeps them alive, a muscle that fails from time to time.

I wander from the yard onto the patio, from the patio back into the yard (it's very big), and finally settle near a railing; below, the gully: several tall trees with thick leaves, some with bright flowers, spreading, sickly-looking, emaciated branches with red flowers at their tip. I cannot bear the noise, the vain pronouncements, the tinkling of the glasses, the smell of mold, of mildew, the silly shadows, the words wafted to me or swept away on the wind, the tyrant jealousy, the vile yet foolish suspicion that comes over me, the evil thoughts (the resentment and suspicion), the hypocritical sentences. I take out a cigarette. I'm about to light it (smokers are at twice the risk of having a cardiac crisis). Are you Nora? I recognize the voice, slightly grave, slightly gloomy, I raise my eyes, a woman is standing before me; yes, I'm Nora, I answer. I haven't seen you in years, she says, I'm glad to find you, because I didn't have anyone to give my condolences to, and her voice changes register: darker. She is a blond woman, tall, her back slightly bowed. I can't quite seem to remember her name. I'm María, she adds. I make a banal gesture, it could mean many things: that I remember her?, that I don't remember her?, that I'm glad to see her again?, that I couldn't care less? Did you visit him? she asks me. I went to the hospital, I say, he was in intensive care, he became very distraught, he had lost so much weight that his dentures were too big for him. He wasn't glad to see me, in fact it infuriated him for me to see him in that state, so sick-looking and emaciated, unrecognizable. It's understandable, she replies, I mean he was so, so-o-o-o handsome. It upset him for people to see him in that state, she repeats, but actually, she doesn't want to hear what I say, she's not interested in what I say, she wants to be the one to talk, wants to tell me her own version of Juan's illness (and death), she says that when he couldn't breathe anymore— strange, right?, she says—he began to wear a moustache, she tells me about him not being able to breathe, about him feeling suffocated, about his pacemaker (one of the inventors of the pacemaker was an Argentine, Favaloro), about the oxygen tank he had to carry everywhere, about the blood clot that went to his lung, about the long needle into his pleura to extract the liquid, about the intense pain that had caused him, about him almost suffocating, actually suffocating to death, that night, and many other nights, about the daily humiliations that make up the life of a sick man: the exhaustion, the depression, the intravenous tubes, the needles, the medicines, the doctors, the pacemaker, the defibrillators (in case of extreme emergency), the angioplasty, the bypasses between the aorta and the coronaries. Her story doesn't affect me, but the way she tells things fascinates me (listen to me with your eyes), the way she moves her mouth, so fast; I no longer understand what she's saying, nor do I care, I'm in a trance, hypnotized, watching the way she spits out her words, frantically, her lower lip beginning to grow thinner and thinner as she talks; her upper lip, much thicker than the lower one, little by little disappears, and just when she says It breaks my heart just to think about it (her lips pressed together in bitterness and resentment) her mouth disappears, she's swallowed it, her face has split in two, a bloody wound slices through it—the edges (lips) of the wound very clear and marked, the wound itself a deep, bright red (crimson?) (that absurd wound that is life)—and leaves a dark trace. The smell of mold, of mildew that follows me, hounds me, haunts me, that surrounded the coffin as though it were a halo, takes up residence now in the scar, and the smell is slight, almost imperceptible at first, then grows stronger and stronger, hot, sickly-sweet. The smell and the wound coagulate, form a viscous mass composed of gestures, expressions, and the repeated, untiring repetition of the word heart. I feel nauseated, my pulse begins to slow (it is now less than 100 beats a minute), her voice rises, the words roll along while I slip and lose my footing and the smell slides down with me, sinks with me into the deep dark hole where the clay revolts. María interrupts her speech, her mouth rests, and when it is entirely recovered (the upper lip fuller than the lower one) (the deep, intense red more temperate), she puts a hand on my shoulder, holds me, looks at me with concern. I make an immense effort, clutch the railing, return to myself, pant a little, calm myself, all within a second. María picks up her last phrase and gets ready to lose her mouth in the process; I've recovered, and I prepare myself to listen to her attentively, but like always, I'm distracted by the asymmetrical shape of her mouth, her upper lip full and the lower lip long and thin, the two pressed together in anger, resentment, or in fear, predestined to disappear: life is an absurd, red wound. A uniform color still outlines her mouth, it's a dark lipstick, a fragment of lip peeks out, then disappears, then appears again, and I concentrate in fascination on the movement and the color: I wonder what it's called—black cherry? crimson? It's a funereal color, it is the only one I know—cyanosis? I stare at her, hypnotized, and I perceive, without understanding, the incessant sound that emerges from her mouth, words uttered at increasing speed, a rhythm quickening, irregular, confused; from between her teeth (white teeth, they contrast with the bright red of her mouth) issues the constant basso continuo (on the cello or the harpsichord) of the word heart.

Then suddenly, abruptly she falls silent, the sound of her nasal voice (like metal) stops. She begins saying goodbye, she leans down to give me a kiss on the cheek, affectionately pats my shoulder, puts out her hand to say goodbye (I speak to you with my heart in my hand, she assures me), mutters a quick condolence. I answer mechanically, and something in what I say—I'm not sure what—stops her, no, captivates her. She looks at me, gesticulates, and as though somebody had wound her up again, immediately picks up her story where she'd left off. Her lips blur, her lower lip shrinks, fades, the design of her face alters, the thicker upper lip takes a little longer to lose its consistency, her face splits in two, swallows her teeth (she looks like Juan when I visited him in the hospital), she eats her mouth, makeup and all, the perfect image of a heart wounded by misfortune, of lips pressed together in anger, resentment, and impatience.

Why do you ask?, didn't I just tell you?, didn't I explain that he couldn't breathe?, didn't you know he was very, very sick?, didn't I tell you that just thinking about it breaks my heart? (Coronography (literally, an X-ray of the coronary arteries) allows doctors to visualize the arteries that feed the heart, when the arteries are injected with a contrasting opaque substance that can, on occasion, produce an allergic reaction.)

They did an angioplasty on him. You know how that's done? A probe with a little balloon is introduced into the femoral artery through a small incision in the groin and it's used to widen the arteries and dissolve the clot (which may be fatal). Then a wire, a metal wire is introduced to prevent a new (and always probable) obstruction. I can't tell you what telling you about this makes me feel, I swear, there's a terrible pressure on my heart (the walls of Juan's heart were thick and rigid, much thicker and more rigid than normal, and the blood didn't circulate well, his lungs were not getting enough oxygen, which is why they filled with water and the doctors had to use the needle to get it out, so very, very painful), you know him, I mean you knew him, you knew him very well, you knew how he was—you didn't?, I can't believe you don't remember. He was proud, very proud, he never complained, never talked about his medical problems, never mentioned his operations or the artificial arteries he had inside him. He spent a long time in the hospital, you know?, medicine is more and more sophisticated, doctors have more and more technological resources for preventing or curing heart disease, but it was too late, his heart was already too far gone, too deteriorated, the heart, we know, is simply a muscle that pumps fluid through our bodies. When we saw him again, after the operation, he was so changed, can you imagine?, he was wearing that sparse, prickly moustache, he couldn't get around without carrying that oxygen tank of his everywhere, yes, didn't I tell you he couldn't breathe? (they say all his teeth were false). A person might think that the heart is made of steel, but it's not, I assure you, our hearts can fail any of us.

Yes, I reply, yes, that's right, his heart failed—you failed me, heart—his heart shattered in his hands (the doctor's hands) (when he operated on him), that heart that once shattered in my hands, life, I tell myself, life, that useless, absurd (red) wound. (I read an incredible article in the newspaper: a French doctor named Marescaux, working from

New York, operated on a patient in Strasbourg. He controls the movements of a robot by using images he receives on a screen (three jointed arms carrying the instruments and a camera), to remove the gall bladder; on the operating table, the patient, totally covered with a sheet (only a very small fragment of his red stomach is visible), and to the side, observing, unmoving, like the figures in Rembrandt's famous painting, three physicians, or anesthesiologists, dressed in light green scrubs, their mouths and noses covered with masks, ready to step in if they're needed.) (Already, remote open-heart surgery has also been performed.) (Artificial-heart transplants have been done: all the patients have died, or almost all of them: yesterday I read that one has survived, he returned to his hometown, some small town in the Midwest, and his friends and neighbors gave him a hero's welcome. The man (in the New York Times photo) is looking out the window of a huge truck driven by one of his sons-in-law, and along the sides, a wall of people applauding, the town band playing a march, the man smiling broadly, his teeth perfect, he's around sixty, how many more years of life are left to him?)

In a very low voice I say to her, Listen, María, how many people have come to the funeral, didn't you say nobody knew he was sick? How did they find out he died? And to think I thought he was going to die alone, like a dog. What's the use?, I think, she isn't listening to me, she never listens, she doesn't want to have a conversation, a dialogue, she just likes to talk, string one sentence after another, once she's started nothing can stop her, she just concentrates on that mechanism that produces words that immediately wipe her mouth from her face: He was in the hospital for so many days, he didn't tell anybody, he didn't feel well at all, nobody knew he was sick, so sick he had almost no heart, and when he got out of the hospital he started using the oxygen tank, and—isn't it strange?—he let his moustache grow out, what was that about? what was he hiding behind that stiff little moustache, as indelible as a tattoo? Incredible, yes, he kept traveling, yes, can you imagine?, *traveling* (on a concert tour?) (how could he manage to play the piano with an oxygen tank sitting there?). I smile, she interrupts herself: What exactly is it that strikes you as funny? No, nothing, I say, pushing a stray lock of hair out of my face—that hair I cut before coming to the funeral, that cut that makes me look young again, that fortunately makes me look young again, nothing, I say, I was just remembering something, but her attention lasts at best a second, she becomes distracted and now for sure I make no effort to understand her words, silly shadows, vain pronouncements. I distract myself by looking at the way she's dressed: she's wearing the latest fashions, with a sober touch that is very appropriate for a funeral—discreet little earrings, light makeup, she's got class!, I think, a good haircut, like mine, and hers makes her look younger, too. I admire her silk blouse, the cut is impeccable, the way it hangs, Armani? (a designer I have wild admiration for, but whose clothes I'm too stingy to buy). Why have I come to this funeral so badly dressed? A pearl-gray pashmina around her neck (maybe shatush, it's very delicate, and on the edge, flowers embroidered in grays (darker than the rest of the fabric, and in the center a red, perhaps cherry-red, dot—like the flower the trees down there have on the tips of their emaciated branches?), yes, pastel pashminas are all the rage now, although the truly elegant woman buys a shatush, with its almost impalpable fibers, it's much warmer than sable, and it weighs nothing!) (why wear a pashmina in such a hot place?). Her shoes are low-heeled, very simple—elegant, perfectly elegant—, her tailored suit is a deep, intense crimson, almost black, perfectly cut (of course) (Emmanuelle Kahn, a label not at all well-known here). She's still talking, babbling, as though life lay in talking, as though she were performing the variations that Marin Marais, the French composer, wrote for the viola de gamba—an instrument used in the seventeenth century for the continuo, a constant, stubborn accompaniment—and that now, at this precise moment, I am hearing, transcribed for the flute, yes, Marais' Folies d'Espagne, whose frenetic, confused rhythm is softened by the thin, intense—stubborn—sound of the flute. That's the way María talks—sometimes her voice is shrill, sharp, sometimes grave, somber. She has a gift for modulating the tones of her voice and making her story livelier, more entertaining. Didn't I say her voice reminds me of the voice of an English countertenor, David Daniels, whose tone is metallic, nasal. I interrupt her from time to time, insistently (tiresomely?), with my chorus: You're right, absolutely right, as my mother used to say, that's right, that's life, life, an open wound. And in a very soft voice I add: And I thought he was going to die alone, like a dog, and as we all know, when the dog dies, the rabies goes with it.

I drift off, free-associate, some of María's words trigger old memories. That time, for example—Juan and I were still living together—, when I was sitting in a corner reading a novel by Dostoevsky (whom I reread often, ritually), many years ago, many shocks, inertias, journeys, deceits, loves ago. In my memories, I am always sitting (today, near the casket, in a chair someone gets up and leaves. María has followed me into the living room, pulls another chair over, settles right in front of me to—insatiably—repeat her story) (variations like those Beethoven composed on an air by Diabelli or Paisiello?, or Johann Sebastian Bach's Goldberg Variations?). Yes, sometimes sitting in the other house, which is very cold, especially in the winter, several of us, friends, sitting, talking, yes, Juan and I having a drink, a glass of wine; other times, we're chatting in a restaurant with several male friends when a bossy female friend with the gestures of a typical barstool macho buys a round of tequila as we celebrate whatever it was, one day, maybe in December, and although nobody wants to drink her drinks, she pulls out a wad of bills like The Idiot (Rogozhin?, when he throws his rubles into the burning fireplace to make his peace with Nastasha

Filippovna?) and we all look at each other in consternation, impotent, the woman's rattling her rattles much too loud, and in the middle of the memory (like the stuffing in a chicken cordon bleu) I hear a few random words from María: ...he spent days and days in the hospital and he didn't tell anybody, nobody knew he was sick, we all thought he'd gone on a trip, like always (with his oxygen tank strapped to his back?), on a trip, on a trip (on a concert tour?, I wonder how on earth he could play the piano with that oxygen tank sitting there?) (high blood pressure, alcohol abuse, cigarettes, sometimes a sedentary life, other things, constant traveling, the hospital, angioplasty, the hospital, open-heart surgery, the pacemaker, the Argentine Favaloro shot himself through the heart). Her monotonous chatter makes me drowsy. My memories keep coming, unrelated, jumbled, the only thing clear is that I am always sitting down, sometimes at a typewriter or a computer trying to tell a love story, or playing the cello, or reciting sad poetry like that poetry by the Chilean poet, or copying the lyrics to some tango and feeling like putting my head down and crying like a baby (eating chocolate cherries, with brandy filling), but I control myself—life, that absurd wound, it is all, all so fleeting—I don't want to humiliate myself and cry in front of María! Do you suppose she'll notice that my eyes are red? But it's stupid to worry about that, she's obsessed with her story and doesn't hear a thing, all she hears is her own voice (Listen to me with your eyes!), she's pronouncing incoherent words that I hear in snippets when my memories are interrupted, and I concentrate on just her mouth, on that scarred-over wound that splits her face in two. She gives a deep sigh, the shadows surround us like an aureola, the silly shadows, the dire yet foolish omens, and the intense (sickly-sweet) smell of mold, of mildew.

Do you suppose she smells it? Or am I the only one?

And I write, I go on writing, sitting at my typewriter... Juan and I were living together; I was helping him type up his writing or copy out his scores before there were computers, when you still had to use different sheets of music paper for each of the instruments, scores, yes, those relics of another time: now everything is written directly on the computer; the race of copyists is extinct, Mozart by candlelight writing out the last measures of his Requiem is obsolete, and Rousseau renouncing the world and devoting his mornings to copying out scores to earn his absurd living (neither absurd nor obsolete—it's an occupation that's simply nonexistent, an utterly forgotten trade). Many things, I tell myself, are obsolete; I smile—how utterly banal! The banality of attending a funeral, of being in the midst of the mourners (mourners? really?)—like just another guest?, just another vulgar guest?

I am sitting in this large, silent, cold room, after listening to Mozart's Concerto No. 20, Köchel number whatever, which has just ended, and yet the stereo is still on—it holds five compact discs—and my friend, the other one, the one from my memory, the one from the restaurant, the one that reminds me of Rogozhin (no, because Rogozhin is short, weak, insignificant—does that matter?), repeats that imperious (though magnanimous) gesture of hers in the restaurant where we're celebrating New Year's Eve—did we celebrate New Year's Eve?—what new year?—Here, I'm the only rattlesnake whose rattles work, she says, and she insists on paying the bill, even if she spends her entire year-end bonus (times of austerity), so we accept, resignedly accept, and we drink and drink until the wee hours. I'm still at the typewriter, or maybe the computer, or in the restaurant with that bossy friend, or next to the coffin listening to María (remembering just then what a singular position she was in): she's going on and on, with less and less mouth, that transverse scarred-over wound, life!, that absurd wound!, its ephemerality, the stubborn murmuring that never stops and that is so incompatible with her clothes. I am still at the typewriter, seized by inertia, or sitting there copying out by hand the complicated scores of Juan's last composition (just as Anna Magdalena Bach, the composer's second wife, did, many of the manuscripts preserve traces of her pen—for example, the most finished version of the six suites for unaccompanied cello. Rousseau, too, when he decided to withdraw from the world, copied music to earn a living, at so much per sheet.) Again there comes to my mind a character from Dostoevsky that often reminds me of Juan, the two of us sitting in front of the fireplace in our house—we were just back from the restaurant after our friend had paid for everyone's evening, and she is sitting beside me, too, or in front of the unlighted fireplace (despite the fact that it's winter and the house is freezing), her Rogozhinian gestures repeating the unforgettable scene in which, to prove his love for Nastasya Filippovna, Rogozhin throws a stack of rubles into the fire, the lighted fireplace in a nineteenth-century Russian drawing room (but no, I correct my memory, it isn't Rogozhin, it's Nastasya Filippovna who throws the hundred thousand rubles, wrapped in newspaper, into the fireplace).

My shoes are black satin, with stiletto heels and an ankle strap; my stockings, dark and transparent, with a seam (perfectly straight); my dress is black, silk georgette with rhinestone appliqués (like a dress to dance tangos in) (I am a cellist and Juan a pianist, and also composer), while our bossy friend, on the other hand, is wearing flats, a thick navy blue V-neck sweater to cover her broad shoulders...she is dark-skinned, her jaw is square, it contrasts with her mouth, which is shifty (and soft). Juan is dressed like a gangster, in a gray pinstriped suit, pearl-gray tie with tiny figures, and a starched white shirt (how can he stand it?, it's so tight around his neck!)

In front of me, María goes on eternally; me, sitting next to the casket or out in the yard (of this house which once belonged to me and Juan and the children and the dogs and cats, or rather cat, singular), or while I read Dostoevsky, interrupting my reading to listen to what she is saying about Rogozhin and the Idiot Prince, everyone sitting—in a corner, in straight chairs and arm chairs of different colors and textures and even shapes, in front of the fireplace that is not lighted, remembering how fast the fire burned up the bills thrown into the fireplace by Nastasya Filippovna, and her lover Rogozhin, who, however, one day murders her (How I wish I were loved that way (in that impassioned way that Rogozhin or the Idiot loved Nastasya Filippovna), even if I were murdered, I think, sitting in my club chair listening to Mozart, Concerto No. 20, Köchel number whatever, for piano and orchestra (especially the adagio). Our friends, all around, are shouting and making fun of my friend the bossy one, and Juan, monotonously and theatrically, insists on reliving the scene in which Rogozhin loved Nastasya Filippovna and to prove his love threw the money into the fire (no, it wasn't him, I tell myself again, it was Nastasya Filippovna who threw the money that Rogozhin has gotten for her into the fire—Nastasya has accepted it; he is dark, small, bilious, with a perpetual, impertinent, evil, and even mocking smile), and in that gesture concentrates all his love, the love he feels for Nastasya Filippovna—the heart has reasons that reason knows nothing of, Pascal wrote. And at that, I weep; before me, the tragic face of María, stopped dead in its tracks as it produced the same repeated word, that wound, that absurd wound that is life, a heart swollen with anger, the heart literally shattered:

(Someone snatches up the bills that Nastasya Filippovna has thrown into the fire; the newspaper they're wrapped in has protected them—only the top one is burned.)

I am sitting in a corner, reading Dostoevsky: Prince Myshkin enters a house in St. Petersburg, looking for Nastasya Filippovna, who has run away with Rogozhin: his heart beats fast, so fast it feels as though it's going to burst out of his chest; in the huge bed he can just make out a silhouette covered with a white sheet, a white oilcloth he later learns. Myshkin feels the beating of his heart (over 150 beats a minute); it is so strong it frightens him, he thinks the sound might go through the walls; the beating contrasts with the funereal silence of the room in which Rogozhin is sitting, no doubt waiting for him—he does not smile. At the foot of the bed lies Nastasya Filippovna's lavish white wedding dress, wrinkled; her diamond necklace gleams on the night table; a foot, clad in lace and silk satin, peeks out from under the spread, statue-like, as though carved from marble. Did you bring the knife with you to Pavlovsk? Myshkin asks. No, I can only tell you this about the knife, Lev Nikolaevich: I took it out of the locked drawer this morning, because the whole thing happened this morning, between three and four. I kept it like a bookmark in a book. And, and this is still a wonder to me: the knife seemed to go in about three inches, or even three and a half, just under the left breast, but only about a half a tablespoon of blood came out on her nightshirt; no more than that. That, that, that, the prince answers, in terrible agitation, that, that I know, that I've read about. It's called an internal hemorrhage. Sometimes there isn't even a drop. If the blow goes straight to the heart.

Rogozhin improvises two beds, the two men lie down next to the dead woman. It is summer, the body will soon begin to smell; Rogozhin has covered it with oilcloth (good American oilcloth, he says) and put four bottles of disinfectant around it (Zhdanov liquid). When they are discovered, the stench will be unbearable, Myshkin will have become the idiot once more, and Rogozhin will temporarily have lost his mind.

It is your death foretold.

Or maybe I'm not reading Dostoevsky, maybe I am just sitting with my legs open playing the cello while Juan accompanies me on the piano (I am now wearing a full skirt, low heels that sit firmly on the floor), we are performing Schubert's lovely, melancholy Sonata for Arpeggione and Piano, I am squeezing the cello between my legs, moving the bow across the strings, the deep sound is a lament, I look at Juan, his right hand moving over the keyboard, his left hand playing the bass. Or maybe we aren't playing, or even together—am I alone?, sitting at the kitchen table that I use for a desk, this dry-green-colored table on which there is a red velvet pin cushion that is a kind of amulet to me, this desk where I transcribe Juan's compositions onto lined music-paper? Perhaps at this very moment a deep sigh has emerged from the depths of my heart, perhaps my eyes have filled with tears (torrents of tears) (burning tears) and then I am really crying—I cry and cry and cry—and now I'm sobbing. No one! I say hysterically, the tears running down my cheeks (they're salty), my heart deeply moved, no-o-o one, no-o-o-o one, has e-e-ever loved me like Rogozhin or Myshkin loved and will eternally love Nastasya Filippovna! The tears run slowly down my cheeks, I like their taste when I swallow them like María swallows her words. I sit motionless, leaning forward, in my lap the face of Rogozhin (or Myshkin) wet between my legs—or is it the cello?—the strings hurt me, and before me, in close-up, the gesticulating and forever open wound—the absurd wound that is life—in the face of my friend. I dreamed that I was lost. I woke up furious!—I haven't found myself (My blood pressure skyrocketed).

I don't want, don't want anyone to realize I'm crying— Oh, I hope María doesn't realize I'm crying!—I'd like to drink my tears, make them return to where they came from, I'd like not to behave like a woman, a vulgar woman, whose heart betrays her. My blood has become inflamed, and from its combustion, vapors have arisen that emerge through my eyes, but no, I will not stand for it, no, I cannot stand it, I am dried out from so much crying, but really, let's not exaggerate, the truth is, it doesn't really matter, nothing really matters anymore, nothing—not my jerky sobbing, not my panting breathing, trying to catch my breath, not Juan's body and his thin, prickly (waxed?) moustache, not the jaw held tight by a black kerchief that brings out the olive color of his face, not the beautiful suits by a famous designer, not the fact that the pincushion is made of red velvet and shaped like a heart, not the fact that the heart (his heart) has stopped beating, not the 100 regulation beats a minute, not the story, not the fact that the heart is just a muscle (the center of life) (if over a long period of time people take constant (low) doses of aspirin (for children) myocardial infarctions are reduced by 44%) (I'd like to die that way, during the night, from a silent myocardial infarction—simple heart failure), nor am I interested in chatting with my bossy friend, who's as heavy as a campesina, or perhaps, better, as heavy as a butcher, standing there among the elegant ladies who have come, like María and I, to the funeral, and the thought occurs to me that youth is a divine treasure, and I hum that tango where the woman is wearing a fox stole and unpolished shoes and a dress that used to be brown and when she was young and beautiful she would recite (with her boyfriend, a duet) the poems of Rubén (I'm talking about Rubén Darío, I hope that's understood).

And the words are heavy when they are written, after I rest my fingers on the keys, in the midst of the silence of the night, only one love like yours has moved my heart this way, my love. I smile—What exactly strikes you as so humorous? says María. Has she seen me crying or smiling? Nothing, I say, I just remembered something, but she's not listening anymore, I hope she doesn't notice that my eyes are red, my pulse racing (more than a hundred beats a minute): it would be humiliating, but actually, I know then (what am I afraid of?) that she doesn't hear or see anything, isn't interested in anything but the movements of her own heart (everybody has their own little heart). (Before me, through the window opening out onto the yard, while I'm writing this story, I see a squirrel pass by, run up into the leafless branches of a tree— it's cold, the middle of winter. I shudder—its tail is the only thing that makes it different from a rat.) María picks up the thread of her story again, hurries to tell that story of hers as absurd as life itself, an absurd wound. You know? (no, I really don't know), you know everybody loved him, such a good-looking, charming man, so pleasant—but why do I need to tell you that, eh? Did you notice he'd let his moustache grow out? Of course, I nod, you're absolutely right, why do you need to tell me, yes, I saw that he'd grown a moustache, it's sparse, gray, useless, yes, some years ago, when we were still living together he was very good-looking. Yes, I know, everybody loved him (although me, I'm still holding a grudge against him—but of course as the tango says, rencor, mi viejo rencor, tengo miedo de que sea-a-ás amor—grudge, this old grudge of mine, I'm afraid it might re-e-eally be love.) And to think I thought he was going to die like a dog, alone, I say (the presence of a pet in the house reduces stress-related tension 50%), and to think I thought he was going to die alone, like a dog, I repeat very softly, or maybe I say it out loud, I might very well have, because this time María does make a gesture of surprise—or shock—oh, that's not me talking, I exclaim (vehemently), not me, his brother said so too, yes, his brother used to say the same thing: When he dies, yes, at the end of his life, Juan will be as alone as a dog (and when the dog's dead, as we all know, the rabies goes with it).

Words, words, words spoken with no connecting thread whatsoever, they make absolutely no sense—or do they? They ought to, they're words that come from the heart and that a person opens up with, even if she shouldn't—isn't that a saying: words can kill? words can give mortal offense? A person develops that mortal instinct, a person wants to kill, words can kill, yes, words wound, words wound the heart, words do harm, do damage, kill—or a person would at least *like* to kill—murder, I mean—with words, especially when they're pronounced with the rhythm at which María is pronouncing them, the convulsive rhythm of gossip, tale-mongering, funeral chitchat—morbid, my God—with her hypocritical sentences whose rhythm is different from the rhythm produced by Glenn Gould when at the end of his life he played the Goldberg Variations and by then was only playing in studios, accompanied by the technicians who helped him retouch the final product, the record that would be sold to music lovers, music lovers who had tapped their feet to the frantically rushing rhythm that Gould used early in his career in his performances of the Beethoven sonatas or Bach's Goldberg Variations—and that caused a scandal at the time. Frantically rushing rhythm: María and her words, a man's heart recognizes them. Words spoken without reflection, with burning imprecision, associations, the way one unconsciously (or consciously) thinks about people's defects, and then, sure enough, when you run into them and chat, although not always, fortunately not always, although often enough, people unconsciously or consciously say what their heart feels, speak some allusive phrase that underscores the interlocutor's defect, and you offend the fat, the bald, the short, the hunchbacked, the beggar, the social climber, the grieving (those who have come to the funeral and talk and talk and talk and gossip and engage in absolute slander, as people will do at funerals—something inside me told me, I just had that hunch. No, says somebody else, his voice raspy, death, as I tell you, doesn't just wander in and speak to us, tell us it's coming—it just comes and that's it, when we're least expecting it), yes, people often utter (hurl) words without thinking, the words just come out of your mouth like *that*, straight from the heart—the heart also has its none-too-virtuous intentions—words resembling the lyrics of that song I was listening to yesterday on the radio—pure heart, broken heart, that Spanish song by Alejandro Sanz (former flamenco singer), that song very popular nowadays that Federica and Corina were listening to in the car as they were driving home, or driving to their father's house, back when they were still visiting him. They're words that just pop out of your mouth, words that come from a heart swollen with grief or anger, a heart that unconsciously unburdens itself, words wielded, by the unconscious—incoherent, parodic, descriptive, realistic, or filled with rancor, resentment, and bitterness (grudges), with the violence of a heart broken not by heart failure but by rage, yet Juan, whose heart was broken so he couldn't breathe or devote himself to pleasure, becomes, or became, a saint—he no longer needs to breathe in order to flaunt his saintliness, because neither saints nor angels breathe, they are entelechies who come down to earth from heaven to shower us with their goodness, they walk slowly and elegantly, with a subtle rhythm, like the hands of Glenn Gould or Gustav Leonhardt moving over the piano or harpsichord keyboard when, with infinite patience and virtuosity, they perform the Goldberg Variations by Johann Sebastian Bach.

It is not unusual, Juan told us one of those nights when we'd get together in the huge, almost always freezing, living room where we would listen to or perform chamber music, or listen to him tell stories with that theatrical (operatic?) voice of his: No, it's not unusual, he said, for a performer, throughout his career, to record the same works several times—the pièces de resistance of his repertory. And there is nothing strange in the fact that one can hear differences between the various recordings (: each performance, each interpretation is different (I think), it shows the various ways the performer has conceived a work, not to mention his or her own artistic evolution—sometimes a performer will change his or her technique itself, the phrasing, the fingering, the way of holding the bow in the case of the strings): the two recordings we have of the Goldberg Variations played by Gould are very peculiar—twenty-five years between them, yes, and with that enormous distance in time, they mark the point of departure and the culmination of his career. He made the first recording in June of 1955, and immediately Gould, who from the beginning had been considered a child prodigy, became the most famous pianist on the international stage, while the second recording, one of his last performances, or interpretations if you will, sainted him posthumously—made him a legend, a performer of truly mythic stature. Each of these recordings holds a special place in the history of piano performances—due in part to the extreme nature of their differences, especially in the length of each recording. Gould explained his theory of length in detail in one of his interviews with Tim Page: I think that the great majority of the music that moves me very deeply is music that I want to hear played, or that I want to play myself, as the case may be, in a very illuminative, very deliberate tempo (Juan stops, dramatically, then repeats as if he were Gould)... As I've grown older, Juan says Gould said, I find many performances, certainly the great majority of my own, just too fast for comfort. (: in order for the heart to function properly one must maintain a certain spiritual peace: it is healthier to be calm). I guess part of the explanation, Gould insisted, Juan insists in a tremulous voice, is that all the music that really interests me, not just some of it but all of it, is contrapuntal music...music with an explosion of simultaneous ideas, and with complex contrapuntal textures, one does need a certain deliberation, a certain deliberateness (like that of a normal heart), and I think that it's the occasional, or even frequent, lack of that deliberation that bothers me most in the first version of the Goldberg. Yes, that record made a huge impact, Juan repeats as he sits, like always, in the high-backed blue chair, the rest of us listening to him (en masse and by compulsion?) with our glasses of tequila in one hand and cigarettes (Marlboros) in the other, the fireplace still not lit, it's cold, Gould's last recording playing mutedly in the background. In almost all his concert tours he would play the variations and then, when he ended all public activity as a concert pianist, one would often hear fragments of them in the broadcasts he prepared for the Canadian Broadcasting Company—to each his own Bach. (I, Nora García, on the other hand, have a special devotion for Sviatoslav Richter as a pianist and as a man—perhaps even more than my devotion to Gould, and I should note, therefore, that in this respect I do not entirely agree with Juan, although Juan may have more standing, as it were, for his opinion, since he was a pianist and I am a cellist. Richter never limited himself to performing the works of just one composer—his repertoire was immense and, as some of his admirers quite rightly point out, he played Bach with all the severity and prayerful modesty of a genius, Schumann with the romantic effusion of a man possessed, Prokofiev with savagery, and Liszt with a virtuosity as refined and phenomenal as only Liszt himself, perhaps, could have attained (Liszt, one of the greatest virtuosos of all time); yes, Richter performed all the composers to perfection and with great respect—he was a protean pianist: Gould was much more obsessive and, above all, much more arbitrary.)

(We are all drinking and having a good time in the living room; the alcohol serves as our fireplace—it heats up the talk and our bodies. Juan, with his scholarly obsessions, does everything he can to freeze our souls.) The decision to record the variations again stemmed from Gould's conversations with a music critic, Bruno Monsaingeon: In my opinion, Gould said, the Variations contain magnificent pieces, although they also contain pieces that are absolutely dreadful (Thomas Bernhard does something similar in one of his books; I have it on my night table—I get so impatient with it: he dismisses most of the great musicians and contemporary composers.) (How different the two pianists are in the way they understand music and performance! Richter played very dissimilar works with equal passion: he was able to find what was extraordinary in each of them, and rather than pulling them down, he raised them up—he exalted them.) Gould capped his (cutting, final, absolutist, inarguable) remark with the following resounding, crushing (and presumptuous) words: As a work, as a concept, that is, as a whole, the Goldberg Variations are a failure (I repeat—I really disagree with Gould and with Bernhard and with Juan.) (The great Romantic composers, those whom Gould scorned (Schumann, for example), would often practice Bach's contrapuntal works every day, in the transcriptions for the piano done by Felix Mendelsohn-Bartholdi, a composer whom Gould admired, although he never included him in his repertory—not him or any other Romantic: Chopin, Schubert.)

(Gould played only in studios, and at the end of his life he hardly traveled, or for example just from Canada to the United States) (Richter, on the other hand, toured a great deal; he preferred to play in small halls out in the middle of nowhere, in French barns turned into theaters, or old Austrian castles, old Bohemian spas, libraries in Bavaria and Ukraine, and, afraid of flying, he would drive back and forth, here and there, in a modest little van, always accompanied by a beautiful piano with a neutral tone, like a white canvas before a drop of paint has been applied (he was a painter as well as pianist), a piano that he'd been given by a famous Japanese instrument company and that had traveled with him on those long journeys from Moscow to Siberia, from whence he would jump off to Japan) (by boat, of course).

Gould intentionally avoided using his first (and highly prized) recording as the point of departure for the last one. He had never listened to it again until three or four days before he began to record the new performance in the Columbia studios where he almost always worked, and from which his most important recordings emerged. A very spooky experience, he said: I listened to it with great pleasure in many respects. I found for example that it had a real sense of humor, all sorts of quirky, spiky accents and so on, that gave it a certain buoyancy, and I found that I recognized at all points the fingerprints of the party responsible (Gould excites me, but he also makes me impatient (when Juan narrates this scene from the life of Gould, I realize that his diction is that of an orator—or that of a city father?), yes, it's true, Gould was truly a genius, but often conceited, arrogant, and fatuous, and Juan would sometimes be just as unbearable as Gould when he took it into his head to explain Gould's theories). It's clear that the young performer, the performer who played

the Goldberg Variations in 1955, Juan explains, might well
have become just another musician, his concerts might have
become bland, colorless, insipid, just another performance.
From a tactile standpoint, from a purely mechanical
standpoint, my approach to the piano really hasn't changed
all that much over the years, Gould repeats (I look at one of
his many photographs: he is still very young, thin, open, a
beautiful head of thick hair, casual, almost, windblown; I
admire his beautiful hands, on the one resting on his waist
one of his fingers is very prominent—long, nervous,
sensitive) (in another photo he is playing, his body bent
almost in half: he has an old man's back (or might it be that
his spine was too elastic?), although he looks very young in
the photograph): My approach to the piano really hasn't
changed all that much over the years; it's remained quite
stable, I would say, static some people might prefer to say, so
I recognize the fingerprints, but—and it is a very big "but"—
I could not recognize or identify with the spirit of the person
who made that recording—I agree, says Juan, interrupting
his discourse (Juan is tiresome, really, so tiresome: I resent
him). It really seemed like some other spirit had been
involved, and as a consequence I was just very glad to be
doing it again. (The squirrel goes by again, its tail brushes
the dry branch on the tree I can see out my window, I interrupt
what I'm writing to look at it, my computer on the enormous
green table in the kitchen that I use as a desk, with a heart-
shaped red silk pincushion on it, the squirrel's tail is thick
and furry) (it makes me feel nauseated) (it is all so fleeting!)
It's an exaggeratedly pianistic recording, and that may be the
worst thing that can be said about any performance (the
squirrel, I see the squirrel), that it seems to boast of its
technique and its strategy, things really, Gould insisted,
absolutely inessential in a true pianist (: life is an absurd
wound, it has made my heart bleed).

What most bothered Gould about his first version of the
Variations, in 1955, Juan repeats, taking a sip of his tequila

and a drag off his cigarette, is the lack of cohesion in the general structure of the work (The memory makes me shiver: his way of telling this story repulses me) (or repulsed me, rather) (Juan's, yes, Juan's way of telling it) (I see that now) (it seems to me the squirrel never finishes passing by the window). The thirty modifications to the main theme (in the 1955 recording) should not yield 30 anonymous miniatures, each with its own movement and peculiar character, but should represent, on the contrary, a logical development, the organic, interlinked growth of a single work. I've come to feel over the years, (Gould added, Juan adds) (Juan and (also) Gould (or their statements, rather) (when Juan narrates them) continue to hammer at me, disturb me, disgust me) that a musical work, however long it may be, ought to have basically—I was going to say one tempo, but that's the wrong word—, one pulse rate, one constant rhythmic reference point. And that is what Gould said, adds Juan, the poor man (Gould) ridiculously bundled up in several sweaters and jackets to protect himself from the cold, despite the fact that the interview took place in July, in the middle of summer (Nastasya Filippovna lies on the enormous bed, dressed in white silk, and beside her body lies the knife, which has but a single drop of coagulated blood, her body covered with a thick oilcloth to hold in the stench: it is summer in St. Petersburg (white nights), four bottles of disinfectant at the four corners of the bed, as though they were candles: Rogozhin has set them out like that, before being seized with fever. Myshkin has reached a state of serenity—a true autumnal peace?, like that which Gould once wished for?)

Obviously, Gould explained, there couldn't be anything more deadly-dull than to exploit one beat that goes on and on and on indefinitely (if the heart should interrupt that beat, 50 to 100 pulses per minute, if that rhythm should change too much, we would die). But you can take a basic pulse, and divide it and multiply it, not necessarily on a scale of 2-4-8-16-32, but often with far less obvious divisions, I think,

(: perhaps here we might use another word, Juan interrupts, and say "audible" divisions) and make the result of those divisions and multiplications act as a subsidiary pulse for a particular movement or section of the movement or whatever and add to its meaning.

I'd like to think, Gould added, in the first interview with Bruno Monsaingeon that Juan quoted (evoked), I'd like to think that in my performances, in what I record, especially in what I've done these past few years, there reigns a kind of autumnal peace—like that peace that reigns in the fields I see from the window of my car, those fields that I (I, Nora García) pass by, in which the sloppily-tied bales of hay are scattered, fields I pass by as I drive toward the town to add my name to the list of mourners who will be going to bid their farewells to Juan. I don't pretend that my last performances have attained excellence, Gould concludes; I would be the happiest man on earth and feel totally satisfied if I could be sure that what we achieved in that recording (the last one) contains just a certain degree of perfection, not just technical, but also spiritual. (I, on the other hand, although I have reached that age, the age of autumn, still do not feel peace, or perhaps only feel that autumnal peace when I have the cello between my open legs and I play Johann Sebastian Bach's suites for unaccompanied violoncello.)

Despite the fact that Gould made other recordings before he died (of works by Brahms, Strauss, and Wagner), the second version of the Goldberg Variations (one must remember that the first recording, in 1955, was done live, at that fabulous concert at which Gould overnight became the most famous pianist of the twentieth century) (nor should one forget that Gould was a child prodigy) represents to some degree his last will and testament, the highest attainment of his artistic wisdom.

As I recall these words of Juan's, I make the same comparison again, and come to the same dilemma: Which type of performer do I prefer, Glenn Gould or Sviatoslav

Richter? The technical ability and immense knowledge that Gould brings to performances of his favorite musicians (but only to them), his expressive intensity yet simultaneous distance, and his strategic ability to gauge the market, make him a genius (that's what Bernhard always said), and yet the wise, modest, although sometimes prideful performances of Richter, the modulations of sharp edges that he employed when he played for example Beethoven—especially the last sonatas, marking the terrible, echoing, yet delicate chords (played with all the strength of his hands and arms), those brilliant registers in the arpeggios that a deaf man alone is able to intuit—make me prefer him. Richter had a particular way of disdaining the market—he rejected publicity, maintained the grandeur yet simultaneous humility of the true artist. He was a conductor yet decided to become just a soloist (in a time when all a soloist ever wanted to do was become a conductor) or, better, an accompanist for a soloist (for several opera singers, for example) or a simple member of a chamber orchestra (performing the trios of Schubert or Beethoven). His hands were magnificent—large, long, powerful, a bit brusque, and they could easily span octaves (although that doesn't matter, a great pianist can also be a small, wizened sort of man with tiny hands, like the Russian composer Aleksandr Scriabin). When Richter played he sat very straight—majestic, stretching his back and arms to their fullest, his feet tense on the pedals. (Fournier remarks that the first time he heard Richter, in the Mozarteum in Salzburg, he realized that his (Fournier's) hands were sweaty and he had butterflies in his stomach, the result perhaps of the great pleasure he felt at hearing a live performance by a pianist whom he had admired for such a long time and whom he'd heard only in recordings until then.)

At the end of our life together, when we would be alone in the large living room of the country house, listening to the recordings of the two great pianists, first one and then the other, Juan and I would have heated arguments that often culminated in violence. Were those, perhaps, two diametrically opposed ways of looking at life? I realized this only later (or maybe it's only now that I'm realizing it, now that with a strange calmness I am contemplating his sallow face displayed in the coffin window).

I'm in Buenos Aires, I've just arrived, I am Nora García: I've been invited to a concert at the Teatro Colón, to hear a concert by Daniel Barenboim. When he comes out on the stage, people stand and give him a long, enthusiastic welcome—the applause goes on and on. Barenboim is not very tall, he's blond (or is his hair gray?, a few sparse hairs slicked down on his otherwise bald head); he carefully, but quite agilely, steps off a little red-painted dais (a step that simultaneously underscores and reveals the worn beauty of the wood that covers the stage), he is wearing a black suit (almost, but not quite, a tuxedo), he waves, cordially but with a degree of surprise; when one looks back on some of the photographs on his records, one sees that he has aged and grown thinner; there's one particular photo that moves me— recently married to Jacqueline du Pré, he looks happy in it, his hair is thick and dark, wavy, lustrous; her hair, on the other hand, is delicate, blond, very long, tied back, although a few stray hairs have escaped, to frame her face: loose ends, golden, pre-Raphaelite; her eyes gleam, her half-open mouth (as though she were in ecstasy?), her slightly moist lips— they are both dressed in the fashion of the late sixties, a time when people preferred to make love, not war (which had not yet ended in Vietnam). He is looking at her as though he were in a trance, entranced, yes, and she is smiling happily: obviously, a happiness so great that it cannot last (: why does so much—and so much!—love die?); in another photo the two of them look as though they are performing (with Pinchas Zukermann) a Beethoven sonata for cello, violin, and piano: the same absorbed gaze, one into the other's eyes (a gaze that throws the violinist out of focus), the same ecstasy, the same predictable, sad future.

The Teatro Colón is full, not another soul could fit in (as the saying goes); many people standing, sitting on the stairs, leaning against the walls of the boxes on the first floor; they are in every possible space in the orchestra, the galleries, the dress circle, the first balcony; and on the upper balcony everyone, without exception, is standing as they listen to Barenboim—leaning on the railing, their heads up among the painted clouds in the fresco on the ceiling, with their antiquated look, their intense azure blue, a blue as blue as the skies in fairy tales. Above the stage, a huge scrim reproduces, in papier-mâché trompe-l'oeil, the red velvet curtains (slightly dusty) that actually begin about midway down the proscenium (which is very high) and that are finished, in a kind of frieze, by a beautiful border in shades of gold that falls in heavy folds on the floor. Above the grand piano (a Steinway?, do you suppose Daniel Barenboim travels with his piano, the way Sviatoslav Richter and Arturo Benedetti Michelangelo did?), and almost the same size as it, hangs a round red-velvet lamp, identical, except in dimensions, to the lamps that lighted the dining rooms of upper-class interiors in the twenties—or lighted the faces, rather, of the guests seated around the table (leaving the rest of the room in modest obscurity) eating (with delicate gestures and not making a sound as they sipped their soup) the food served on Art-Deco plates. The lamp reminds me of the red silk pincushion that is always beside me (an amulet?) when I write—sitting on the huge kitchen table (olive green) in the other house, where Juan is telling us, with his wonderful diction (maybe a little exaggerated—operatic?), about the conversations Glenn Gould had with Tim Page and Bruno Monsaingeon. At the Teatro Colón, the curtains framing the stage and the lamp crowning it look like they've been made of the same rich velvet that Scarlett O'Hara used for that revealing low-necked red dress she seduced Rhett Butler with in Gone with the Wind (we are so poor, says the man taking tickets at the door as we stand in line for the elevator that will take us to the fifth floor (he is a tall, fair-skinned, elegant man with gray hair, a handsome, masculine face: a prince in exile?), we have so little money that we haven't even been able to buy toilet paper for the bathrooms: the trash men and cardboard-recyclers pick the trash up in front of the theater, from a trash area protected by a fence, the same kind of protection that will be protecting the streets near the Plaza de Mayo the day after my visit to the Teatro Colón: metal chain links and an endless wall of police officers will be blocking the way to picketers).

Barenboim plays Beethoven's Sonata No. 3; he will be giving 8 concerts, and will perform (from memory) all the sonatas (32). The movements are fast, the technique very good, but I remain unmoved—I am much more moved when I think (while I sit in the hall listening to the pianist) about Beethoven, remember that when he composed this sonata he had not yet become deaf: we know that because of the precise sound of the chords, the neatness of the trills, the acrobatics of the hands as they run up and down the keyboard—the left hand leaping over the right to play the melody—the echoing arpeggios: Barenboim's left foot gleams when it presses down on the pedal: from my seat I am looking at him from the front: when he completes the first movement of the sonata he stops, takes a dark handkerchief out of his pocket, dries his perspiration, while people move about in their seats and begin to cough as though a conductor were conducting them. When silence falls again, he picks up the second movement with great brio, the spectators rock in time to the melody and lean against the railings in the balconies to see better, then close their eyes and abandon themselves to ecstasy: when the last chord dies, everyone stands and applauds furiously: from the fur coats of the ladies there comes a strong smell of moth balls, which soon pervades the hall.

At nine years of age, Barenboim left Argentina with his parents, and he returned almost forty years later—yet as he himself confesses in an interview in which his Spanish flows at first with some difficulty, though in an Argentine accent, he recalls very clearly the smells, the colors, the location of buildings and plazas, those beautiful buildings and plazas now gone to seed, at the corners of which garbage is piled so that the cardboard-recyclers, legions of the ragged poor, can classify and recycle it.

All time, all moons, all blood reach a place of stillness: the Teatro Colón still bears the traces of its nineteenth-century splendor, and there, from one of the seats in the dress circle, I, Nora García, who is a cellist and who was once married to Juan (who is now dead and was once a pianist), am listening to Daniel Barenboim in one of the concerts at which he will perform Beethoven's 32 sonatas in the Teatro Colón in Buenos Aires. Daniel Barenboim, a pianist who was married to Jacqueline du Pré, a beautiful, famous English cellist who died (very young and at the peak of her glory) of multiple sclerosis, a cunning disease (on one of her last records, she still looks radiant, ecstatic, embracing the cello deliriously (she is playing Saint-Saëns' concerto for cello), but one can already begin to see the traces of the disease in the slight imperfections of her bowing, as the arc of her instrument presses on the strings).

Am I once again hearing Juan's emphatic voice? Is that possible? On May 29, 1981, at a little after midnight, when Gould walked out of the Columbia recording studios located at 207 30th Street in New York City (a former Presbyterian church), a chapter in the history of recorded music closed forever, as did the final chapter of the career of producer Samuel Carter, a promoter of Gould and many other famous artists. Because the Goldberg Variations was the last record officially recorded there: Columbia—the Mecca of the great virtuosos—was about to be sold, a victim of the changes of fortune in an industry which, like any other, was reeling from the onslaught of the multinationals and international competition. For Glenn Gould and for those others whose fortune had been linked for so many years to Columbia, the former church is a place haunted by ghosts, said—the epitaph for his own company—Samuel Carter. That recording might well make Gould another of those ghosts (unquestionably immortal), Juan concludes: in the background of the immense living room, very softly, can be heard the last recording Gould was to make of the Goldberg Variations.

Beginning and end are joined, as in the esoteric symbol of the Ouroboros, the serpent that bites its own tail, the perfect allegory of the Infinite, and also of the Eternal Return (: as though one were to say wrestling with the angel). An angel with a heart literally broken in pieces, a heart only a small part of which remained healthy, a heart destroyed by disease, not by love, a damaged heart (the heart is simply a muscle) with portions of it in a very bad way, with its one, two, three, four, five bypasses (roads rerouted) done in several emergency operations, acts of salvation, the reconstruction of bridges and roadways, because the blood circulates without ever reaching the river, it is detoured without correctly purifying the lungs, despite the fact that the arteries and veins have been reconstructed or cleaned out or new arteries or new veins have been grafted in, with new road signs, so the blood can be routed as it should be to all the parts of the body—the legs, the belly, the hands, the fingers, the eyes, the nose, the brain, and before all else, purified, to the lungs—or does it go to the heart after purification in the lungs? A heart wounded by seeing so much misery? I must find out whether those roads are winding or straight (each year, more than 50,000 people die in France of heart attacks, and 300,000 in the United States—how many, do you suppose, in Mexico?), these roads go from one place to another, like all roads, but what is one to do if the heart is broken in a thousand pieces, the mitral valve doesn't work (or the tricuspid?) and the lungs have water in them and the bridges that span the lakes are falling down, falling down, and a massive heart attack occurs? (Men are more susceptible than women to heart attacks) (a needle in the lung, in the pleura, to drain the water from it is perhaps one of the most terrible pains a person can experience—perhaps worse than childbirth).

If a myocardial infarction occurs, a portion of the heart dies and what is left intact is just a piece of muscle—a tiny part of that wondrous muscle—and that brings on anxiety, angst, the impossibility of breathing, of motion, difficulty in climbing stairs at home or on planes when one goes on tour, because planes require travelers to have a heart that is whole, a heart of steel, not a heart that is broken, with two parts useless or dead (now all sciences are struggling in unison to save the precious organ, the organ of life, the organ of emotions, our heart, yes, all the sciences in unison— chemistry, biology, physics, genetics, engineering): the impact produced by the myocardial infarction obviously leaves the heart without its myocardium, or splits it in two, like María's face, María's shattered face, or Juan's heart shattered by the heart attack (if those problems are not addressed immediately—problems of heart rhythm—the possibility of survival plummets; in fact, if within four minutes of the heart attack's occurring aid has not arrived, that is, if the heart is not reanimated, the brain, deprived of blood flow, sustains irreversible damage), the heart attack shatters and splits the heart, leaving only a portion of it healthy, though fragile, and preventing the body from abandoning itself to its pleasure, that body now no more than skin and bones, because one now hardly eats at all, and despite everything smokes and smokes and smokes (and drinks, mainly tequila) (Herradura Reposado) and despite everything drags a tank of oxygen around and runs the risk of dying of respiratory failure. Life is an absurd wound, and everything is so—fleeting!! When the heart becomes ill, it loses its gleam, its shine, the membranes become congested and an inflammatory serum seeps toward the central cavity (to avoid this, one must live a healthy life, not eat polysaturated fats, dress salads with olive oil, eat nuts, dates, almonds, vary foods, use salt in moderation). At that moment, the parietal and visceral layers rub against one another each time the heart beats—and if the heart doesn't beat, the body dies—and friction is produced in the front part of the chest, which can be heard through a stethoscope, and even by percussion. (Semi-automatic defibrillators increase the average chance of survival from twenty to fifty percent; in some places they're known as idiot-proof because anyone can use one—just push a button that sends an electric shock and the heart begins beating again, $250,000, the price of a life!) (Life is an absurd wound!). The heart, the organ of life, seat of the emotions and therefore of the soul, symbol of love, yes, the seat of life and emotion: at first, heart surgery devoted itself to repairing genetic deformities, most of which can now be operated on: valve surgery is a large percentage of that work (valves taken from animals—pigs or cows—are used) and also metal valves. One must recognize that this type of surgery has its limits, and that after eight or ten years calcifications tend to appear, which must be operated on. The anatomy of the body, and especially that of the heart, points us back to the great myths created by humankind, life and death, the origins of humanity, and its future. Sometimes when the covering of the heart is torn, and the covering of its casing is broken (the silk lining of my cello case), the mechanical functions overlap, the heart atrophies, and the heart simply stops. Right?

Is that what happened?

Did his heart atrophy?

The heart is protected by the sternum and the ribs, and also by the pericardium: an incision is made in the middle of the thorax, underneath the sternum. The bone is sawed through (bone dust flying) and the pericardium appears— the membrane that surrounds and protects the heart—then the damaged coronary arteries appear. Another surgeon prepares the graft (often part of the saphenous artery (from the leg is used) or a mammary artery is detoured from its natural course). The heart is taken out of the thorax and laid on the sternum (the right part of the sternum): it is hard to operate on a beating heart; a special procedure known as extracorporal circulation is employed (using a device specially made for that purpose), it does the heart's work and sends blood to the entire body (especially the brain) during the insertion of the graft: the graft is attached to the aorta on one end and on the other, placed under the obstructed coronary artery. Once the operation is completed, the heart is replaced in the chest, and the regular movement—diastole, systole—resumes immediately, the blood flow is reestablished, a vascular bridge has allowed the obstacle to be bypassed. After the operation, which lasts from two to five hours (depending on the number of arteries repaired) (or on the surgeon's skill) (up to five bypasses can be done in each operation), the patient remains under observation for several days in intensive care, before being sent to a regular room. At that moment, the process of rehabilitation begins.

He's going to die like a dog, alone, I repeat, aloud, when my interlocutor has left, he's going to die as lonely as a dog, yes, as a dog—when the dog dies, the rabies is over. I wish he had died like a dog, alone, but he didn't, he died in the company of many, like a hero, followed by many dogs, male and female (bitches), men, women, and children, he has become an angel, a pure and marvelous entity that leaves its mark, a red mark in the eyes of men and women, in my eyes, in the eyes of María, in the heart of the mourners, profoundly moved: Juan has left an immense void in the nation, a void impossible to fill, an immense void in the history of the national and international music world, he has left unfinished the work that he did so well, searching for lost and misplaced scores and manuscripts, traveling from museum to museum, from one musical archive to another, journeying from Vienna to Berlin, from Berlin to New York in search of manuscripts and scores, manuscripts and scores that would allow him to show in his lectures and books that Bach was different from

Pergolesi, although Bach died quietly at home, setting down notes one after another, composing cantatas, tempering his harpsichord, his well tempered harpsichord, the harpsichord on which many nights Bach, to amuse himself and amuse his family (his second wife and their children), would perform his own Goldberg Variations, composed for a student of his, of that name—Goldberg—who in turn, also every night, would play them in the home of his patron, Count Keiserling, a nobleman wracked by insomnia. Pergolesi, on the other hand, died very young, of tuberculosis, in his bed, foreshadowing the Romantic way of death, that Romantic way of death that obliged Schubert to die of syphilis and Schumann to descend into madness. And Bach composed partitas and fugues, cantatas and masses, concertos and chorales, and made children, twenty, though with a change of wives, because the first one died in childbirth—, but his sex drive was overwhelming, doesn't the number of his progeny prove that?, did he not have twenty children? (ten survived). Or perhaps it was simply the unvarying schedule of his daily life—quiet, impeccable, systematic—compose partitas or fugues during the day, play them on the organ in the evening, teach the sons whose voices have not yet changed the songs sung in the choir (as Bach himself had been taught when he was a boy), those fragments of the cantatas that he had composed, and then, at night, naturally, of course, at night, at night devote himself to making children. Bach, a quiet, normal composer of steady, rhythmic, domestic sexuality, like the chords on the harpsichord in the Goldberg Variations when Wanda Landowska performed them on the harpsichord, or when, about to die of a myocardial infarction, Glenn Gould recorded them on the piano, differently than he had performed them when he was very young, overnight becoming a legendary pianist, the great pianist who in two concerts—one at the beginning of his career in a public recital and the other at the end, in a recording studio—performed the same Goldberg Variations at a totally different tempo, a totally different speed: in his first concert, he performed them with astonishing swiftness, in 37 minutes, and that same recording (the 1955 recording) includes excerpts from the second book of the Well-Tempered Clavier, one fugue in F-minor, and another E-major, and the four pieces together lasted barely 46 minutes, 11 seconds! And to think that the rhythm of the heart is from 50 to 100 beats per minute! That the heart also expels 5 liters of blood every minute and there are 100,000 arterial and venous vessels carrying blood through the body! Slowness, however, must have been Bach's legacy: the last recording of the Goldberg Variations that Glenn Gould made in 1981 (at that point in his life when he no longer went on concert tours and recorded only in specialized studios—the Columbia studios—and was soon to die of a myocardial infarction) lasts 51 minutes and 15 seconds—14 minutes and 15 seconds longer than the first recording, which made him famous! And the harpsichordist Gustav Leonhardt—who thinks that Bach's Goldberg Variations (BWV 988) are indisputably one of his most extraordinary compositions, written at almost the end of his life—performs them at an even slower tempo, in 54 minutes and 19 seconds! (100 beats a minute!). The variations were conceived as exercises, discipline for the performer, and they represent an incredible advance in the canon of the fugue and its variations. Variation 30, which Bach called the quodlibet, was, as Juan explained it to me (I had read this, too), a cause for rejoicing for his family when he, Johann Sebastian Bach himself, performed it for them. It's true, Bach composed his cantatas only with great love, and with great love he also impregnated his wives—the first one, who died, and then the second one, who survived him—those awkward composers' wives who kept suddenly dying in childbirth, or soon after, of puerperal fever, Juan said, smiling. Yes, Bach almost certainly made his children with love and passion, Juan explained, before his heart became diseased (Juan's)—does the heart of man not recognize the virtues?, is the heart not simply a muscle? And he, Juan, would add: How else could Bach have had such talented children, famous composers who outshone their father during his very lifetime, those children begotten upon his first wife, the one who died in childbirth: Wilhelm Friedemann, his favorite, the talented but insecure and introverted firstborn, and Karl Philip Emmanuel Bach, much more famous than his father, and, at last, another of his offspring, also quite famous, although this one the child of Anna Magdalena, Johann Christian Bach, who was fifteen when Bach died? Have artists not been given an enormous gift (a divine gift), the gift of being able to read the hearts of men?

The heart has reasons that the intelligence knows nothing of. Among the Egyptians, the heart's weight determined the dead person's guilt or innocence before the judges of the dead. Embalmers would take the heart out of the body, place it in a separate vessel, and in the place of the heart put a sacred insect (a stone scarab). Medicine has made great strides, especially in the area of angina and myocardial infarcts. If a coronary artery becomes obstructed, sufficient circulation of the blood, and its oxygenation, cannot be ensured, which is the reason that today true underground constructions are employed, which function like on- and off-ramps, counteract a deadly process of degeneration, because when the mitral valve doesn't function, for example, the circulation is rerouted, forced into new, artificial routes, and that causes terrible damage to the heart, congests the lungs, and shortens life enormously. I imagine that Juan suddenly had an attack of nausea that left him exhausted. Perhaps, making a superhuman effort, he managed to hold himself up against the wall of the little street he was walking along. The pain must have been unbearable, a pain never felt before (it was, perhaps, an irreparable pain), and he may have realized that he was lost, that his heart had been ripped apart and that he was going to die like a dog, alone. But no—a stranger who happened to be passing down that same little street came to his aid, called an ambulance to take him to that hospital where many days later I was able to visit him, see him, now so thin (his dentures were now too big for him), and with that sparse, gray moustache and a befuddled expression in his eyes, because now, for sure, Death was whispering in his ear.

At home, I listen to the music of Bach, always the same record, the Goldberg Variations performed by Glenn Gould—his last performance, the one that lasts 51 minutes and 15 seconds—, and my thoughts wander as I follow the rhythm, a slow, quiet, persistent rhythm; the music is arithmetical, limpid, although that limpidity, that clean progression tends to blur when Gould insists on accompanying—humming along with—the austere melody. I open my eyes. I have not moved from my chair. I am near the coffin, I stare at Juan's yellowish face. I turn my eyes away, and there are scores scattered everywhere, on the table, in some of the chairs: before, yes, before we parted, Juan was very neat, he kept his scores perfectly filed in the file cabinets, but now they are scattered around the immense living room, beside the wreaths or among the flowers, on top of the grand piano (a Bösendorfer with a score on the music stand), on which a cello is propped—by me?, do you suppose it has some recollection of that time, those sessions when we would play a Beethoven or Haydn sonata together, or Schubert's Sonata for Arpeggione and Piano (he at the piano, I at the cello) or when he—Juan—would perform the Goldberg Variations on the harpsichord? In the living room there is a harpsichord with the top open, decorated with idyllic pastel-colored paintings. There are violins, too, one or two violins—a Stradivarius or an Amati? Too many violins for someone who played the piano, I tell myself, stupidly. Flowers, flowers everywhere, on the floor, in wreaths, in vases, next to the scores, and, despite everything, despite the fragrance of the tuberoses and the heavy smell of the candles and these memories that wash over me and distort me and that I hum, I cannot rid myself of that smell of mold, of mildew, it encircles me like a halo, like those silly shadows, those dire yet foolish omens, those aureolas that circle the heads of saints in paintings and statues.

Poor Pergolesi, on his deathbed, Juan would say with emotion in his voice—would it have been that night when, after celebrating New Year's Eve, we had come back from the restaurant and were sitting in front of the unlighted fireplace in the other house, with that bossy friend that imitated Rogozhin's gestures?, or maybe it was a Christmas night and we may have celebrated New Year's at home instead, with a glass of champagne, I in a black silk dress and very high heels, Juan in a gray gangster-suit and his shirt collar unbuttoned. Pergolesi dead so young, at twenty-six, disenchanted with life, shortly after his opera L'Olympiade was performed in Rome in 1735, a resounding failure. Can you imagine, Juan would say, imagine?, he would repeat, taking a drag off his cigarette: At last—touched by the hand of greatness, Rome, the capital of art and opera! Poor Pergolesi, he was always hounded by bad luck, Juan would go on, and we would sit absorbed listening to him because he knew he told the story well (told it in his own way, and as though it were a fiction invented at the very moment he was telling it; he really did try, and often succeeded—as a result of his research—in revealing the secret lives of his favorite composers, one of his obsessions: dig into people's private lives). I read it in one of the memoirs that was never known until just a short time ago, he says, after taking a sip of tequila—I found them in a castle near Pozzuoli where Pergolesi was buried—they say that in that Roman theater (the Teatro di Argentina) he spent several days rehearsing with the singers and orchestra, rehearsing his opera, the opera he had composed in the most fervent, even impassioned state of mind—was it not to be performed in Rome?, had he not become a famous composer? A composition he had to alter later, however—forced by the whims of the divas and castrati that were the darlings of the Roman opera-going public, and when he did so, when he made the changes to his score and added special arias so that the particular tessitura of each and every one of the singers could be appropriately displayed, a scandal broke out—instigated by the conductor and his enemies, Pergolesi's enemies, the members of a cabal. The performance of L'Olimpiade (which was the name of the opera by Pergolesi performed in Rome, the libretto for which had been written by the famous Metastasio) was abruptly interrupted, and to catcalls, whistles, boos, and rotten tomatoes (etc.), the audience stormed out of the theater. The composer, inconsolable, his pride profoundly wounded, sitting at the harpsichord, bows his head into his hands. Yet when the theater is deserted, silent, a bouquet of red roses falls onto the stage. Happy the musician!, the memoir said, and Juan repeated it enthusiastically, happy the artist who lives to receive such a reward, a bouquet of roses tossed by an anonymous admirer! Yet Pergolesi never recovered, Juan goes on (do you suppose his heart failed?), as we all, spellbound, sat listening to him—sat in the chairs in the living room where his coffin has now been laid out. Shortly afterward, Juan says, taking a drag off his cigarette (now a Marlboro light) and holding his glass of tequila in his other hand, like all of us who were listening to him then and who now sit beside his coffin in his house, Pergolesi died, his heart wounded by misfortune, died in Pozzuoli, a little town far from Rome, the capital of art—died, of consumption!

Life is an absurd wound, and it is aaaall, aaaall, so— fleeting!!

And in this living room they are sitting beside his coffin, here, where I myself am sitting, beside his coffin, too, with María's wound-face before me, endlessly repeating the same endlessly repeated story of his death, the death of Juan who was once my husband and my colleague (Oh, my aching heart, what evil curse is upon thee!), in this very living room where Juan would rehearse his works on the piano: he would play a fragment, a few bars, and then stop to bend over the ruled paper and write the notes on the stave, as once Schubert had done (and Mozart and Beethoven and Pergolesi too). Juan would sit for six, seven, eight hours at the piano, playing and transcribing onto the scores the notes he invented, and Schubert would do this, too, shortly before he died of syphilis, the heinous disease. Juan would use a Mont Blanc to write his notes on the pentagram—he always would, except at the end of his life, when he preferred to use a computer. Computers have changed things, now everything is simpler with a computer, the music of each instrument can be written automatically, you don't have to use separate pages for the violin or cello or flute parts, yet when his periods of calm set in and he wasn't traveling madly about the world, freeing himself of who knows what excesses, Juan would often write lovely variations and note them directly on the stave, following the grand old tradition of Bach and Beethoven (whose scores are covered with erasures and scratchings-out, notations written in a crabbed, convulsive, incomprehensible hand), compositions written especially for us—so that together, we two could play here, Juan at the piano and I on the cello, my skirt very full, my open legs holding the cello tightly, as though it were an inexorable, hard, inflexible (merciless) part of my body. Yes, Juan would first write his compositions on stave-lined music paper, but then he started doing it on a computer, because things change and time passes and one no longer needs to know how to write music on music paper (as Mozart had done, at night, in the light of a dim candle, or Rousseau, copying scores to earn a living, at so much a page), all you have to know how to do is use a computer, read music on the cybernetic staves, and then print them and listen, through your headphones, to the music you've composed—an automatic, instantaneous process, actually, which is why María says that Juan used to say that if there had been computers back then, Beethoven's fate would have been quite different—Beethoven, the musician whose most perfect symbol is the oxymoron, a composer who can't hear what he composes, or, better, a musician clinging to the ineffable sound of the music of the spheres (Gould preferred to play Beethoven's early works, the ones he wrote before he went deaf—which are precisely the works that for so many other performers are even better, more perfect, than those Gould favored) (although one of those Gould played was perhaps the most romantic of all: Claire de lune!). Modern science is truly modern, and one can immediately hear, yes hear immediately the music that one composes directly on the computer, or one can scan the music that other composers played or composed and that were transcribed onto scores by Bach, Pergolesi, Händel—composers that Juan liked, and Mozart and Schubert, too, especially Schubert when Juan rehearsed his impromptus on the piano.

The heart has mysterious ways that reason knows nothing of, even if the heart is actually just a muscle, like the muscles of the legs and hands. I see a cello in the living room, not far from the coffin (it's perfect) (a Stradivarius?, I don't think so, it would be too expensive, since Stradivarius made only a few cellos, but many violins) (it is reddish, and it gleams, and its body is soft, voluptuous), well, it's logical for there to be a cello, there was always a cello—isn't the cello my instrument?, did I not live with Juan for years?, were my heart and his not one? (one single impassioned heart?). What's not logical, on the other hand, is for him to have violins (why wouldn't that be logical?—he was a conductor, after all). Flowers, flowers everywhere, on the floor, in wreaths, in vases, on the piano, next to the scores, not on the harpsichord, though, because its top is up and you can see the delicate, romantic-looking scenes painted in pastel hues. A heavy smell makes it hard for me to breathe, the smell of tuberoses combined with the odor of the candles and with these memories that wash over me and shake me and that I hum (like Glenn Gould when he was recording the Goldberg Variations in the Columbia studios), I cannot, cannot rid myself of the smell of the flowers, but especially the smell of mold, of mildew: it hovers about me like a halo, like those halos that encircle the heads of saints in paintings and statues.

I have listened to so much music these past few days, these terrible end of the year days, and I have wept so many tears of grief and bitterness (black tears), I have wept so much as I listened to the music that I cannot go on listening to it, I cannot bear it, I am saturated. I begin to soften, the tears pull me down, carry me down to the deep dark hole where the clay revolts (Juan now has a crucifix held in his arms, on his chest, on top of his heart which has stopped beating) (: with love, or during the absence of the beloved, blood rises in waves toward the heart: the effervescence produced by its combustion makes vapors rise to the brain and, from thence, to the eyes (the windows of the soul), become vapor (compare their transparency to the thickness and color of the blood): when the cold of sadness retards the circulation and the flow of the vapors, a subtle alchemical reaction transforms them into tears (what poetry rightly calls the broken heart) (between his hands). No doubt about it, I will have to spend several days in silence because a person's emotions become drained, worn, withered, and I can no longer relive the sensation, so sadly pleasurable, the immense melancholy, the tearful tenderness, the violent spasm that goes from the throat to the heart—that noble, courageous, energetic organ, the heart, organ of emotions, organ of passion, an intense emotion that pierces us, or that pierces, moves, wounds the heart, makes it bleed (hot, bleeding wounds to the heart), an emotion I can capture most faithfully when I listen to a miraculous combination of notes in certain passages (only in certain passages) of Bach's cantatas (the series conducted by Nikolaus Harnoncourt) (the sudden change from major to minor), performed almost always by male voices—the countertenors, tenors, basses—but especially by the boys that sing in the choir and, sometimes, as happened in Bach's time (his young pupils were charged with singing the female registers of the composition) (women are not to be heard in church), as soloists. It is them, the young soloists, that I am fascinated by—I am moved by the young singers, much more than by the perfect voices of singers when they are mature, the professional singers. The sound truly pierces my heart, the ephemeral sound that emerges from the throats of the boy singers of Vienna, Hannover, or Tölzer, a shallow voice that barely vibrates, a brief moment, during that time when their voices are still adolescent, trembling, uncertain, intact, emerges before the physical changes that occur during puberty darken their register. I idolize with (all) my heart and with (all) my soul that sharp (piercing), thin timbre (crystalline and fragile), that childish (and therefore angelic) register (the testicles have not yet descended, and the larynx has not yet become seated, Quignard remarks), voices emerging from bodies whose sex is tremulous, innocent, delicate, different than the bodies of men, who are beings with hard voices and defined sex, radically different than that of the boy singers of Vienna who sing (sometimes just that bit off-pitch) when they enter a dialogue with the mature singers (the bass or tenor) or when they sing an aria as soloist (the change of voice is an illness of the voice which is cured only by castration). The intonation of adolescents, a voice that approaches—though does not attain—the feminine. An indecipherable voice, the voice of boys that sing like boys, with their hearts in their hands, before any physical change has altered their anatomy and their register and transformed them into beings with somber, masculine voices—men, slaves forever to their age and their sexuality.

Men trained in the art of falsetto, the countertenors, sometimes manage to equal the female voice (never the voice of boys)—actually, their voice is different than women's, although they imitate it: there is always, down there somewhere, within the belly or the chest, hidden, powerful, a trace of virility. Why that insistence on the part of countertenors to sing like women or—if they could—like boys, or (what a wonder that would be!) like castrati. Can the forced, strident voices of falsettos compete with theirs? (Boys'?) Yes, I ask again, why do they want to sing like women?, is it out of nostalgia? (as though they wanted to anchor themselves in that intermediate time of their lives, before their body was entirely subject to sex or age?). The castrati's great originality stemmed from the shape and position of their larynx. It is true that after the change of voice, a man's larynx descends, like his testicles (: the voice parallels the sex), but the castrato's remains anchored to its original location in the throat (to that physiology he had when he was a boys) (changes can occur even in women, a slight change of voice) (with menopause?), which is why the vocal chords of the castrati remained located closer to the resonance cavities, with an effect of height and brilliance in the register and great clarity in the timbre and a greater range of harmonic sounds. Why were castrati so fashionable?, why did they exert such fascination?, why do countertenors now want to imitate them?, are their bodies and faces not quite masculine?, why does a female (feminine) voice emerge from their throats? If it were just poetry or sensitivity one were looking for, one could find it in those singers, the normal singers, who have spent their lives restraining, subduing their voices, learning to modulate them, to sing in delicate, violent, heartwrenching, or simply daring registers, but no, I am convinced (I would so have liked to hear them) that the voice of the castrati was sublime. I, who am a cellist and who appreciate the somber, intense tones of my instrument and of the human voice, prefer to listen to the boy singers who perform Bach or the baroque composers, singers often inexpert but whom I (I insist) put at the very pinnacle of my list, for in their voices the flesh, sensations, spirit, instinct— all that comes from both the physical and the spiritual— mingle in subtle, tacit accord, in precisely the way clouds in the blue sky are tinged with blue. When those young boys sing the arias of a Bach cantata their voices quiver, vibrate for a single instant, an invisible instant, denoting a peerless register of voice that pierces them and us, transfigures them and us: they have become incorporeal, angelic beings (although sometimes they are a bit off-pitch or cannot manage to reach the highest notes), they are pure entelechy, like Juan after his death, transformed into an angel that illuminates our lives. Yes, that is the fragile, quivering (asexual) voice of the boy singers of Vienna when they sing a Bach cantata with the members of the choir or when they are soloists (when their voices eclipse the other singers'). And it is at that instant, the instant when I listen to them sing an aria or modulate a recitative with their fragile, tremulous voices and as they strain to reach a high note, that imperceptible second, it is at that instant that I am moved, moved so deeply that I begin to tremble or sob: of course I don't begin to tremble or sob just because their voice may change (although that moment is worth a sob), I begin to tremble with emotion because the voice of the little boys who are singing in the choir have an imperceptible tremor and underneath that tremor is hidden what their true voice will be, the voice that will define them for the rest of their life, that dark wound that is life. But the voice of the boys is ephemeral, it is so fleeting, they cannot preserve forever those delicate, pristine registers. Although perhaps their voices can be preserved, or rather are preserved, held forever (forever?) in the imperceptible groove of a recording, and when we hear them played we experience once again that delicious sensation, the sensation produced by the sweet, tremulous, angelic, and ephemeral voice of the boy singers: now I, Nora García, am listening to such a voice—it is a Bach cantata conducted by Nikolaus Harnoncourt. That is the voice that breaks my heart, the young of the boy singers who, if they continued to sing—only if they continued to sing—would later sing as tenors, basses, or baritones, that is, sing like men who devote themselves to the cultivation of their voice, the deep voice that will assume the registers of the tenor, the baritone, or the bass but that will never, ever

again attain the delicate female (feminine?) registers they
reached when they were boys and one could still read their
heart like an open book, that heart always true, shattered in
our hands. Although—why not?—the nostalgia for that voice
might lead them to become countertenors, so that from their
virile, bearded countenances might emerge sounds similar
to those they sang when they were boys, with that antique,
fragile voice, sometimes pierced before its time by a
prophetic register of masculinity.

One of those evenings with friends (were we never
alone?) that took place in this very (enormous) living room
in the country house where Juan has been laid out—me not
looking my best in pants and boots and a too-heavy sweater,
or elegantly dressed in a low-cut black dress, fishnet
stockings, and high heels (: in the living room of the other
house, the house in the city, in winter, with the fireplace not
lighted)—Juan is narrating an episode from the life of
Rousseau, an episode from Rousseau's youth, when he was
working as secretary to a French ambassador in Venice. One
day Rousseau (when he had not yet withdrawn from the
world, when he was not yet earning a living copying music at
so much a page), Rousseau, I say, or Juan was saying,
Rousseau was listening to a choir made up of little girls from
an orphanage in Venice, adolescent girls who sang like
angels, and he had but one desire, one fervent desire—to
meet those girls, even if he had to violate the rules of the
convent; a friend tries to dissuade him: You'll be
disappointed, he tells him, and you may even regret it. And
still, Juan repeats, and still Rousseau insisted on meeting
them, seeing them with his own eyes, those eyes that were to
be eaten by the worms, as, within a short time, when he is in
his tomb, the worms will eat Juan's eyes. And indeed, what
his friend predicted would happen did happen: when
Rousseau has the girls before his eyes, face to face, when he
looks at them, none of the little orphans matches her voice:
one's face is ravaged by smallpox, another has but one eye,

that one over there is a dwarf, and this one here is unimaginably ugly, but when they sing behind the chorus, hidden behind the screen, their voice is like the voice of the angels, angels who are indeed utterly beautiful, in both body and soul, yes, the girls from the orphanage that Rousseau visited were like angels when they were unseen, when one only heard their voice behind the chorus screen, girls who sing (or sang) like the boy singers in Vienna, Tölzer, or Hannover sing, or sang, in a recording that I always listen to, a recording that has preserved for eternity the register of a voice, captured at an ineffable instant, when the boy singers still sang like angels, like the cherubim with deformed faces that Rousseau insisted upon meeting: the angelic voice of the boy singers of Tölzer have been preserved forever through the technological miracle of a common, simple compact disc—a voice identical in its androgyny to the voice of the orphan girls that Rousseau met.

The first movement of the Sonata in D major D.850 is too impetuous and impulsive, quite unusual in the works of Schubert, Juan explains to us, changing (musical) subjects, after Christmas or during New Year's Eve, as we sit in the enormous living room drinking champagne and smoking, beside the unlighted fireplace (although it is very cold) where our bossy friend is dozing off, the friend whose feverish gestures imitated those of Rogozhin as he threw money into the fireplace—that fireplace, indeed, lighted—of an upper-class drawing room in nineteenth-century Russia, a scene masterfully recounted by Dostoevsky in The Idiot, which Juan so delighted in remembering (though he altered some of the scenes). The rhythm of its principal theme, the theme of Schubert's Sonata in D major, Juan underscores as he sits in the high-backed blue chair and loosens the light gray silk tie that is squeezing his neck, that theme, he says, dominates the entire work, and each of the variations is engendered by the preceding theme: Juan stops his story, makes a theatrical gesture with his right hand, sets his glass on the little table beside him, picks up a cigarette (always a Marlboro light), takes a drag, and after a masterful, almost pianistic silence, picks up the glass again, stands up (his suit is cashmere, charcoal-gray with white pinstripes) and picks up his story with the implacable, infallible logic that characterized his conversation: Schubert modulated a few strange chords that reappear suddenly in a much slower tempo (on the manuscript, there is a notation—capriccioso—in the composer's hand). And when the central theme is performed, the chords repeated from the first theme undergo an amazing transformation, and Schubert, Juan explains, used the strident call of a hunting-horn—performed on the piano! (what a splendid idea!, impossible to improve upon), an actual hunting-call that returns in the coda in a much faster tempo than the rest of the movement! Against the slow movement he juxtaposes a melodic theme—very brief—, Juan underscores in a very soft voice, and then it changes, it takes on a syncopation, lighter, much lighter, angelic, and ends in a series of arpeggiated chords that slowly disintegrate, so that what results is a harmonic sequence almost Wagnerian in its audacity, but then that, too, suddenly, once again, fades away (just that unexpectedly, without warning) and there emerges an infinitely painful sigh, from the very depths of the heart. When the main theme returns, Juan says, at the same time standing and going toward the piano, the Bösendorfer—yes, it has to be a Bösendorfer—and when he reaches the piano he explains the way the pianist's right hand plays the main theme while the left plays the role of a violin or a viola da gamba, as though it were a basso continuo (which was played on the cello), allowing the piano to achieve sounds known in musical jargon as portamentos, or expressive glissandos, very romantic (totally different from those Gould achieved in those moments when his performances reflected only an autumnal peace). When Juan plays the fragment again, one can clearly hear the contrast, a theme impetuous yet finally very intimate—an echoing intimacy that triggers within me, in the very depths of my heart, an intense feeling of happiness—at once painful and pleasant. This impassioned work that Juan loved to perform is surprising despite the modesty and innocence of the theme of the rondo—surprising for its delicacy, yes, a delicacy that compensates for the peremptory rhythm of the previous movement. Schubert is definitely delicate yet audacious, and that was very clear when Juan performed him, as it is clear to me now, too, when Juan is dead and I am listening to the performance of the work that András Schiff recorded on this disc with a green cover; only they—Juan and Schiff— managed to make the notes of the sonata fade away, little by little, in a slow finale whose rhythm softens and calms the grief and allows slow, sweet tears to rise to the eyes from the very depths of the heart.

András Schiff, for his part, explains a striking and unusual fact: only recently has Schubert begun to be recognized as a great composer for the piano and not just a writer of lieder: Juan knew this, of course, before we bought the recordings of Schiff, a pianist who has become fashionable after his death (Juan's death). Some of his other works for piano (Schubert's) were hardly ever played. Juan would often compare them with Bach's Well-Tempered Clavier or Art of the Fugue, or with Beethoven's 32 sonatas, incomparable musical monuments, the pinnacle of genius, within the history of art and music. Juan felt that Schubert's piano music has the same importance for the piano repertoire as the work of Chopin (or Liszt) (and—although to a lesser degree?—the work of Schumann) has had—a fact long overlooked, so overlooked in fact that several of the pieces that Schubert wrote for the piano were not heard until long after his death, that early death caused by syphilis. Juan insisted—playing the same fragment from Schubert's Sonata No. 17 in D major D.566 on each of the pianos, that is, first on the Bösendorfer and then on the Steinway—that it is a sacrilege to play Schubert on a Steinway, which is unquestionably a marvelous instrument, but too objective (perhaps) for those delicate sounds, and he (like Schiff) recommended using a Bösendorfer Imperial, that same piano that I see from where I am sitting—before me—in the huge living room of our old house, as I sit beside Juan's body laid out in state, the body of Juan, the pianist, composer, and conductor with whom I once shared my love life and my musical life. Yes, in this living room one can admire a Bösendorfer (with its scores on the music stand), an instrument which, Juan would monotonously repeat (and demonstrate with a few chords from Schubert's posthumous impromptus), has a much finer and more expressive sonority than the Steinway or the Petrof—yes, if what one wants is to perform the work of the Viennese composer, Schubert, with sincerity and mastery (and we performed them together so many times, especially the Sonata for Arpeggione and Piano, transcribed for the cello), then one must play them on a Bösendorfer. Music performed on a Bösendorfer has greater tonal quality, a quality demanded by the piano works of that famed yet unfortunate Viennese composer. No, definitely, Schubert cannot be played on a Steinway. Schubert sounds the way he should sound only on a Bösendorfer. (And, by the way, where *is* the Steinway?) To underscore this statement, Juan would interrupt himself in a chord, stand up, and put a compact disc (with a green cover) by András Schiff on the player (Sony). It is a Bösendorfer on which Schiff performs Schubert's posthumous sonatas (D.566, D.784, and D.850), written by him shortly before his death, in the flower of his manhood, a year after Beethoven died and Schubert, carrying in his right hand a torch and feeling every toll of the bells in the Vienna cathedral echo within his heart, took part in the grand procession by which that city paid its farewell (with profound emotion and solemnity) to the deaf composer of Bonn, that extraordinary teacher (of Schubert, of Schiff, and also of Juan).

Unless I'm mistaken, it was in the Royal Festival Hall, in

London, a concert by Arturo Benedetti Michelangelo, the hall full, the conductor English, I can't recall his name, perhaps very famous, the piano a Bösendorfer, brought over from Italy by Harrods especially for the occasion, and with pride evidenced in the program itself. We've flown in from Amsterdam, the Italian pianist is one of Juan's favorites, and Juan is especially interested in hearing how Benedetti Michelangelo interprets Beethoven's Concerto No. 5. Benedetti Michelangelo was one of the most enigmatic and capricious of pianists (because he would often cancel his concerts) on account of his demands, his temper, and also perhaps because he had been Mussolini's pilot during the Second World War, which is not exactly a high claim to glory, although the way he performed the Romantics certainly was—his astonishing, infinitely varied fingering, the contrast between his hands and his face, his elegant, delicate way of phrasing the melody. The pianist's hands travel over the keyboard and are reflected in the instrument's cantilevered top—his thin, nervous fingers vibrate, tremble, modulate— he is dressed entirely in black, with a cashmere turtleneck, a white kerchief with which he wipes the perspiration from his brow; his movements are rapid, staccato, arrogant, he raises his very thick left eyebrow, his straight, exact hair gleams slightly, a thin moustache above his thin, sharply-drawn mouth. The conductor moves the baton doubtfully, nervously; Benedetti Michelangelo inhibits him, he ignores the conductor's movements, forces him to alter the rhythm, to follow the rhythm he sets, he conducts him from the piano, his smile glacial, correct, the smile of an English duke on whose face one would have seen firmly printed the exact impression of the vowels, the arrogance of the consonants, the scornful and always stiff upper lip. Hardly has the last chord sounded when suddenly the applause erupts— endless—the audience has risen to its feet, and there is shouting, almost howling, the conductor applauds furiously, he is carried away, swept up, he perspires. Benedetti

Michelangelo, tall, thin, bows slightly, his hand on the piano. The conductor: an Italian amateur who, to seduce a lady, once burst into an aria from Puccini in the middle of the street.

Arturo Benedetti Michelangelo introduced to music, life, and love another extraordinary pianist: Maurizio Pollini.

Juan looks at me, caresses my face with his hand, takes my arm, and we find a taxi to drive us to the airport, on our way to Glyndebourne, in Wales, where we will attend the annual opera festival, will hear (and admire) Händel's Xerxes: in a leading role, a famous countertenor, David Daniels, a man with a masculine face and the voice of a mezzosoprano.

(... in the middle of the recording of a concert performed by Emil Gilels, Schubert's posthumous impromptus, one can hear people coughing: it was impossible to eliminate the sound, it was a live recording. In Gould's recordings the audience doesn't interfere, he always recorded in the Columbia studios in New York or Canada, and although the performer demanded that the final version be perfect (and he would edit it like a film, to achieve an impeccable recording), Gould could never erase his own voice, that monotonous murmur, that humming that accompanied the melodies of the pieces he played. Music lovers who admire Gould have no choice but to hear that irritating sound when they listen to his recordings—that rasping, throat-clearing sound that Gould produces. When he plays he forces upon us his style of playing, a style which despite everything is, for some music lovers, the sign of his genius (Thomas Bernhard), that quality of performance that sets him at a place much higher in the pantheon than that of other virtuosos (a celebrated pianist such as Bendel, Bernhard says, when compared with Gould, is simply a fraud).)

This living room is no longer neat, no longer orderly—papers are lying about on boxes, on shelves, some scores on chairs, others up on the Bösendorfer's music stand: did those orderly, neatly copied-out scores not demonstrate that Juan was an upright, august man, a hero of the profession, a statesman and leader of the vocation, a magnificent pianist, an extraordinary composer, a zealous and meticulous researcher—a man with heart!—in a word, a man who, on the day of his death, will be accompanied, like Beethoven, by thousands of anonymous people, and by friends, true friends, to show the world that a man shall not die alone, like a dog (or like poor Pergolesi who died at twenty-six, alone and crippled, yes, crippled, because Pergolesi was not just tubercular, he was crippled)? Pergolesi, a musician admired by Juan and his contemporaries, but looked down on in Rome by music lovers and other composers who, envious, persecuted him and then, after his death, recast his arias and enjoyed resounding successes in all the theaters of old Italy. But Juan, unlike Pergolesi, was very popular while he was alive, although probably he was not as talented a composer as the Italian. Juan is followed, was followed by all, yes, Juan was recognized in life (that absurd wound which is life), Juan was visited by many friends, and Juan is now being buried by those same friends, whose faces are distorted in grief as the coffin is lowered little by little into the grave, a grave prepared beforehand, empty, but which will be filled at the end of the speeches, the crying, the ringing of the convent church bells that echo in one's heart, the wracking breaths, the tyrant jealousy, the creaking of the coffin that moves out of position and that four men straighten again, before the holy water is sprinkled on the body, holy water that looks as though someone had scooped it up out of some filthy puddle, and someone, I can't see who, tosses a large white flower—it falls on the coffin of rough white pine, and then I remember—how could I not remember?—that rose or bouquet of flowers that fell onto the stage when Pergolesi was weeping over his failure. And then they begin—the bunches of flowers, flowers and more flowers—gladiola, white roses, red roses, yellow roses, crepe myrtles, carnations, daisies, calla lilies, poinsettias, tuberoses. Some of the flowers are fresh, others wilted, and their fragrance mingles with the smell of the candles that people in the procession are carrying (the hot wax melts, falls, burns their hands) and for a brief moment the tuberoses, especially the tuberoses, mask the sickly-sweet odor of mold, of mildew, that has been following me since we left the house and that now, halted with me, as though it were a halo, encircles me as I stand at the edge of the grave and wait for the body to be brought. The sun dazzles me, I put on my sunglasses because one's eyes cannot (without being blinded) bear to look directly at the sun, or at death.

We have walked the entire way from the house to the cemetery, a cemetery located in the middle of the valley, and during the entire procession the smell of flowers and candles has never overcome the dirty smell of mold, of mildew that hounds me and haunts me, that washes over me and that perhaps only I can smell, perhaps follows only me. (Do you suppose the smell of the body of Nastasya Filippovna, stabbed to death, was masked by the four bottles of disinfectant? Four open bottles of Zhdanov liquid, Rogozhin explains to Prince Myshkin.) And people look on, their faces distorted in grief, their hearts shattered, and no one is making jokes anymore, those jokes they were telling in the yard at his house, my old house, while the mourners drank their tequila, and now they are standing beside the grave as the mariachis have fallen silent and those who spoke the solemn last words of farewell have fallen silent, too, and now stand very gravely next to the grave, without spilling a single tear, because men do not spill tears. All that can be heard is the crying of the children and the old women (who dab at their noses with their aprons) and the barking of the stray dogs. Yet Juan, Juan has not died like a (stray?) dog (like the dog in his house, who died after giving birth, splayed out on the floor, her teats black, falling on the floor?), no, he has died as a hero, he has become an angel—so thin, not an ounce of fat, consumed by the illness, his heart had shrunk, had lost its muscle mass, and now it had hardly anymore to give, his breathing became labored and he needed an oxygen tank to be able to walk, his quality of life changed, he couldn't go out at night as much as he had, couldn't travel, do his research, give lectures in his theatrical (operatic?) voice, let his hair down, live large and free, not caring about the illness or the pain or even death, with his heart sullied, his heart that had no very virtuous projects in view, a constant squandering of strength and libido, open, immediate desire, vile polymorphous perverse suspicion (which is how psychoanalysts describe the Marquis de Sade, whose libido was of an immense polymorphous perversity), like the figure in the drawing I'm given later, a drawing done in strong, simple lines that depict a man, his legs open, his phallus erect, disproportionate to his body, the image of desire transformed into pure, almost philosophical erection—Heideggerian, one might say (if one were to turn philosophical)—and around the man with the enormous phallus are other men and women, much smaller of stature, more sickly-, rickety-looking, and they are the recipients of his erection, mere repositories for a desire in which the flesh is outsized and pleasure gigantic and the scene is grotesque, almost ominous, but fascinating in its naked carnal vitality. Yet they are all drawn with a few pencil-strokes, the sketch of a figure with its legs open, equivocal, dozens of sex organs, a huge penis that emerges implacable, impeccable, and one end of it penetrates the sex of a much smaller woman, who is lying on her back with her legs open, and another woman looks on in open-mouthed admiration, looks at that genitality drawn in utmost nakedness, in a few skilled strokes. One would say, nonetheless, that the drawing is not correct: the name of the artist is written backward, as though the man or woman who had drawn it were totally drunk or (a man) copying onto the drawing a scene in which his body has become a long phallus, making his body a single long shadow, as long as the one in the poem: a trace. And the male organ, says León Hebreo in his Diálogos de Amor (Dialogues on Love), León Hebreo too says it straight out, without fear of vulgarity, in the pure and impeccable Spanish version by the Inca Garcilaso de la Vega, that great writer and chronicler, the son of an Inkan princess and a soldier who was the descendant of another great poet—the male organ, I write, copying down the words of León Hebreo (Yehuda Abrabanel) that Juan would read to me as we sat in front of the unlighted fireplace in the other house, unlighted despite the cold, the male organ, Garcilaso says León Hebreo says, and Juan would repeat it and now I am transcribing it here, the male organ is proportional to the tongue with regard to posture, and in the figure and in its extending outward and retracting back and in being set in the middle of all and in its work and motion, and just as by moving the male organ bodily generation is effected, so the tongue engenders spiritually, and the kiss is common to both, the one inciting the other.

And I remember the kisses of his mouth, the taste of his tongue, I, Nora García, and she, Nora García, remembers and weeps, or rather a few tears come, which she discreetly wipes away, different in this from men who cannot shed tears, because men do not shed tears—men, as we all know, don't cry. She has not brought a handkerchief that would allow her to cry elegantly and wipe her eyes delicately, no, she uses a vulgar Kleenex, a Kleenex instead of a little embroidered handkerchief that Juan may have given her so long ago, or that I—she, Nora García—gave Juan, and on whose fine white linen cambric his initials were embroidered with my hair and that she, Nora García, has (I have) hidden among the love letters that he once wrote me. And Nora too, I repeat, Nora has wept, I weep like a baby when I am auscultated, examined, analyzed, for fear that in my future, or hers, Nora's, there may be a tumor that will have to be operated on, and then a death—to die, ominously, as alone as a dog. Do you think Nora García is not fighting it, do you think Nora García is not fighting? Fighting that man that is no longer what he is or what he was, that is no longer Juan, that can no longer be Juan, vain shadow, because he, that body that was once his, is even now being eaten by worms?

There is a painting by Caravaggio of a concert, and in it the performers each carry an instrument, place their fingers on the strings of a guitar, a lute, a theorbo (: from the Italian tiorba, teorba), a zither, or a mandolin, and one hand holds a bow, placed on the strings of a violin or a viola da gamba, and to the lips of some of the performers in the painting are held a transverse flute, or a trumpet, or an oboe, and while the players play, forever young, their lives stopped at the precise, stubborn instant they are playing their instrument, one can see on their faces the slight tremor, the blink, that incipient flinch, or wince, or contraction of the muscle (the beginning of an ecstasy that will be silent?), an absorbed though brilliant gaze, the look, the blink, the tremor accompanying the movements of each performer, for example those of the almost-child castrato playing an enormous archlute—a figure that is common in the paintings of Caravaggio, a young man who sang as a child in the choir of an orphanage school where boys were recruited to be castrated so that their voice might remain forever that of a child. Can one read in the gaze what one feels in the heart? Does truth peer out of the eyes, is it revealed in the expression of the face, in the expression of the mouth, in mine when I play the cello or when Juan played the piano, or in the expressions of the young musicians portrayed by Michelangelo Merisi da Caravaggio? Can a castrato express himself with sincerity? Are the eyes not the windows of the soul? Can grief be read in the mouth of María, who disappears as she talks? Can a mutilated face tell the truth? How is one to be truly sincere if the organ that produces the sounds (or the colors) cannot be seen? Are the crude colors that Caravaggio used in his paintings true?—those colors that he achieved by use of a lantern that alternately lighted and shadowed his models, those young men of clear, quavering voices and faces with rosy cheeks—angelic yet perverse? The heart of a person insensitive to the pain of others, incapable of experiencing the emotions of goodness, turns to stone, but God can save us through a transplant of the spirit. The castrati resembled angels in all their features, Juan explained to us that same long New Year's Eve, and he explained this after telling other stories—the story, for example, of the deformed girls in the Venetian orphanage whom Rousseau once heard sing. In Neapolitan conservatories, did they not dress eunuchs as angels to watch over the bodies of dead children? The castrati perfectly matched the aesthetic ideal of the time—the eighteenth century—in almost all of Europe: they were objects of contemplation, of veneration, compared with the angels, linked to the traditional figure of musician-angels, and so they embodied (because of their voices much more than because of their acts) purity and virginity. In the Church, thanks to that voice that seemed to defy earthly laws, the castrati were viewed as holding a privileged place on a line that connected God, music, and humankind. Is there anyone who has not used the word "angelic" to describe Allegri's Miserere, that work written by a castrato to be sung by other castrati? And finally, were they not the most perfect expression of that baroque art which portrayed angels, one of its most symbolic figures, in sculpture, painting, and music? There is a contradiction in German with respect to the word alto, the voice of a contralto. Alt also means old, but boys, girls, and women do not have to reach maturity to sing the parts written for the alto or the contralto. The word is derived from the Latin word altus, high, and we might say that to define the voice of sopranos we can use such words as jubilant, exultant, joyful: the voice of a true contralto is characterized by its warmth, its exuberant lushness, and especially by its coloratura, whose radiant tones turn velvety and dark—the way María talks—and I listen to her in fascination when, sitting beside me, in that chair near the coffin, she enthusiastically and in great detail describes the processes that accompany death.

In the circle of countertenors that have come onto the market, most of them from choirs in English churches, to become soloists, there is one exception—René Jacobs—who would be an exception if only because he comes from Belgium, although he is also exceptional because he has found, in addition to and beyond sacred (interiorized) music, a vocal art that expresses great dramatic intensity, the vocal art that was the glory of the castrati of the seventeenth and eighteenth centuries. Gifted with a voice which extends from the highest notes of the mezzo to the low notes of the chest register yet which always, even in the lyrical repertoire, retains its masculine timbre, he is able with equal facility and perfection to take on the virtuoso parts intended for the castrati of baroque opera as well as the simple, intimate singing of more recent times.

The castrati of genius were the absolute monarchs of eighteenth-century Italian opera, and they inspired a wild enthusiasm and devotion, sometimes fanaticism, in the public even beyond the world of opera. Although the falsetti, if we may call them that, could be found all over Europe, they had fallen from fashion, despite having been the predecessors of the castrati, because they sang using just their head voice, a voice that is extremely clear yet sometimes imperfect, masculine.

It would no doubt be an exaggeration to say that, save for England, the arrival of the castrati brought about the fall of the falsetti as soloists in the profane repertoire. Often, even in Italy, falsetti would pass themselves off as castrati, but they would be discovered because they had offspring, which convincingly proved they were not eunuchs. In England, castrati and falsetti openly interchanged roles; they would have the same roles as the female contraltos. Händel exploited this interchangeability when he composed certain roles for his oratorios—the singer would be determined by the particular circumstances of the performance. Fortunately, Händel wrote his compositions for castrati in the register of mezzosopranos. Eighteenth-century opera and theater increasingly called for this sort of vocal transvestism, and for an increasingly larger number of singers able to perform both the male and female parts. This fact constantly led to comic situations: on one occasion, after a double change of roles of differing sex in a single scene, the English countertenor George Mattocks sang the part of Achilles dressed in female clothing. The staging was the determining factor. Most of the castrati had the stature of Greek heroes. The female singers, however extraordinary they might be, never had either the voice or the stature to rival them (despite the makeup, the high-heeled or platform shoes, the costumes). Nor did their voice have the impressive sonority of the high-range male voices that the castrati preserved and enriched, despite their emasculation. Now, as in the eighteenth century, the voice of a countertenor is probably that which best reproduces the voice of a castrato—the voice of David Daniels, for example.

I wander again through the yard, my mind turned inward, my body haloed by the smell of mold, of mildew, and by the sound of words brought me on the wind, words I cannot make out—the words rebound, echo, tattoo, come from several groups scattered about the space...they are scrambled, confused, but at last I make out, clearly, a few words theatrically delivered with very rapid diction, they approach, come closer and closer to me, I hear them now very close by, they have been spoken by a woman standing in the middle of a small group of people, she is holding a glass (of tequila), a well-dressed, sober, elegant woman, her suit by Emmanuelle Kahn, dark gray or perhaps a coffee color so dark it looks black—black cherry, perhaps? (Shops exist because vanity is immortal.) She's seen me. María leaves her friends, rushes over to me, and as I watch her approach, cigarette in her hand, still far away, from far away, she begins to modulate her voice, begins to repeat, hurriedly, in her beautiful voice, the customary words (when she modulates her somber voice it reminds me of the voice of an English countertenor, David Daniels, the singer whose voice—as I imagine it—is the closest approximation to the voice of a castrato, his voice different from the timbre achieved by male voices because of its lightness and flexibility, and different from the voices that emerge from the throats of women because of its brilliance, limpidity, and power, and superior to the voices of children because of its developed, total adult muscularization, its technique, and its expressivity), and María's words recompose, in a wealth of details, the story of his death, the story of Juan's death. Her face is still intact, her features visible, her eyes (I hadn't noticed before) a curious color— in novels or poems they are often called glaucous (or are her eyes as dark as oblivion?)—, her nose thin yet prominent, scattered freckles covering her face, which is covered only partially by makeup slightly darker than her skin tone, her lips red, outlined with a darker pencil—crimson, almost black, like the color of her black-cherry-colored suit, a designer suit, probably by the French designer Emmanuelle Kahn, who is almost unknown in Mexico. Her teeth are very straight and white, her tongue pointed (what other shape could such a talkative woman have?) (Juan had lost all his teeth and it was hard for him to talk: those long stories he would tell in that loud, operatic voice that could reproduce in detail Glenn Gould's conversations with Bruno Monsaingeon). María is agile, supple, her step elastic. He could no longer breathe, breathe, brea-eathe, she repeats, the oxygen tank, oxygen tank, oxygen tank, everyone loved him, respected him, admired him, he was so handsome, he spoke so well, he was so wise, recently he'd grown a moustache— a sparse, gray, prickly (waxed?) moustache (now she is shouting, everyone turns to look at her): he was such a wonderful pianist!, so seductive!, so handsome!, at the end he couldn't breathe!, breathe!, brea-ea-eathe!, brea-ca-

71

eathe!! (The heart is simply a muscle that pumps blood to our body.) Her lips as red as blood (which has stopped circulating in Juan's body) gradually disappear, leaving a thin, gummy trace, a small, sinister scar, an absurd wound, life. Hypnotized, I hardly hear her words, or see the people who surround us, me: everything, everything, everything disappears, and nothing, neither noise nor the out-of-tune singing of the mariachis nor the deafening vibrato of the trumpets, can blot out the admirable luster of her voice— similar, I conclude, to the voice castrati had.

María, unfazed, recounts several scenes from his death: I concentrate and with some effort manage to catch a complete sequence, a sequence that María rushes to tell in her metallic, nasal voice. The difficulty he had breathing, María says, meant he would have to interrupt himself in the middle of a concert, or gasp for air if he tried to walk a little faster. One night he felt a pain under his sternum that eroded his chest and made him feel first hot and then cold, a pain accompanied with a slight rattle in his breathing. Then he felt like he was fainting, and a terrible, terrible pain shot through his chest, his arms and legs went numb, so he decided to call an ambulance. He was alone, and he didn't tell any of his friends. He spent several weeks in the hospital, totally isolated (and with no teeth), or he may have been visited by some of his closest collaborators. (Connected no doubt to several machines whose tubes and wires tangle on the floor and walls, transmitting to strategically located and variously colored screens a graphic, epileptic representation of his state at every moment, the mad line of arrhythmia: the crazy beating of his heart.) María's breathing becomes labored, pained as she tells the story: in the hospital, she says, he began to cough up this viscous fluid and his pulse became unstable, so the doctors decided to do open heart surgery on him (the Aztecs believed that human sacrifice, that ancient, primitive practice that prefigured modern heart surgery, was necessary for their survival).

María interrupts herself, makes a sign with her hand, and a woman comes over, it's her friend, she says hello to María, to me, and with one of her eyes she studies me fixedly (rudely), her other eye is blind, the pupil occluded by a whitish film. Wow! I tell myself, this is more like a circus, a curiosity shop, a museum—maybe, why not?, even a fashion show than a funeral! The one-eyed woman is also very elegant: she is not wearing an eye-patch, and the bright eye contrasts strikingly with the cloudy one—you can't see the pupil, or it might be better to say that the pupil doesn't let light through, and that opacity, I think, forces her to express the truth with just a single eye—are the eyes not the windows of the soul? Or maybe the woman doesn't speak the truth with either of them, or, too, a banal association that now occurs to me, her veiled eye, her cloudy eye, may be the one that can best reveal her. Does open heart surgery turn the heart transparent again? How can we know whether the love others profess for us is sincere? Music doesn't lie, we know that perfectly well—we feel it, there's no getting around that, we feel when an instrumentalist performs a piece well (do you suppose it's possible to read a score with just one eye?), we know that the instrumentalist performs it with feeling, that it is with the most authentic passion that he or she performs a work for piano or violoncello or any other instrument, or for the voice, although here I prefer to talk about the instruments I know best, those that Juan and I played together—he, the piano, I the violoncello. I repeat, I reiterate: I think that when someone performs a piece of music well, we know that it is totally sincere, we know it because that person has managed to transfer his or her own emotions to the instrument, thereby translating and communicating the composer's emotions, or what the performer thinks are the composer's true emotions, whether those emotions have been expressed serenely or tempestuously, slowly or convulsively—the way, for example, Glenn Gould, still very young, performed Johann

Sebastian Bach's Goldberg Variations in just 38 minutes, 27 seconds, or the way pianist Sviatoslav Richter (who won his first musical competition at thirty years of age) (completely different in his musical career and in his way of playing the piano from Glenn Gould) performed with such perfection a huge musical repertoire, unlike his contemporaries, or the way someone on the cello, such as Mstislav Rostropovich, performs Marin Marais' Folies at lightning speed—Marais, a French composer who composed for the viola de gamba, an instrument now obsolete, similar to the cello. We know, intuit, that his emotion is true, it comes through in the sound, that extraordinary singing, that harmonic progression that the performer wrings from his instrument, and know too when someone cries—do we know it, really, do we? Tears, those obvious manifestations—if they are real (how to prove that?)—of the most absolute sincerity. But if they are, if tears are sincere (and not crocodile tears, as the saying goes), yes, if they are real, then tears go beyond words—words, apparently faithful reflections of emotion yet capable of betraying emotion and distorting reason. In that impalpable instant that makes the motions of the heart visible—or better, audible—emotions are falsified, become deceit, deception— a rhetorical deception. Is it impossible to express passion? How is one to break down the barrier that the body itself imposes? How to do so if the heart is simply a muscle? How is one to see, touch, what the heart feels? The heart shattered in your hands? My heart was inside his, his inside mine.

Juan wrote down his compositions and played them on the Bösendorfer (the way Schubert did during the last years of his life, when he was very ill, in the hospital, his health destroyed by syphilis). Juan would compose beautiful compositions in the grand tradition of Bach and Beethoven, compositions specially written, at first, so that we two could play them here together—he and I, in this living room where we are now sitting beside his body in state—Juan sitting at the piano and me playing the cello, in a very full skirt and my legs open wide and the violoncello like an inevitable part of my body. The cello which was once a filler instrument, used only for the basso continuo, the continuo ostinato—wonderful phrase, the eternal and ongoing state of obstination. By Schubert's time, the violoncello was beginning to be a solo instrument (wait, let me clarify, that statement is not entirely true: Bach used the violoncello for his variations for unaccompanied cello and Marin Marais also composed for the violoncello, although he was actually a composer and virtuoso for the viola da gamba, a kind of cello, a predecessor of the cello). In the Romantic repertoire the cello was used as a basso continuo in concertos and symphonies, and when Schubert wrote his Sonata for Arpeggione and Piano, the cello (in this case, the arpeggione) was not yet a solo instrument...it took the cello a long time and some effort to free itself from its servile role as accompaniment, ostinato continuo. With Viennese classicism the cello truly began to be used in orchestras as a solo instrument, like any of the other solo orchestral instruments: the violins, the trumpets, the French horn (which is called the "English horn" in Spanish!). The brilliant, expressive, clear registers of the cello seem to emerge from the soul itself—the cello is the most human of the instruments, it can reproduce the sound of the human voice at the exact moment the human being is feeling the most profound grief. Yet the enthusiasm the public felt for the cello did not actually have much influence on composers, who continued to compose to showcase other instruments, the violin for example: the repertory for the cello grew only slowly, which is why the virtuosos who most often played in private drawing rooms and concert halls had to take up the pen and write their own compositions for the violoncello, or transcribe them from other instruments. It would be impossible now to cast Schubert's Sonata in D major D.821 out of the repertoire, despite the fact that it is not composed for the cello, strictly speaking, but rather for the arpeggione, an instrument that was first constructed and used in Vienna around 1820 and at the time was known as the guitar-violoncello and was played, like the true cello, by holding it between the legs, although its shape and number of strings—and, therefore, the sound produced—were like a guitar's. An interesting combination, a hybrid—similar to the voice of the castrati?—an artificial combination which by its very nature was destined not to last. I was and am a cellist, as was Jacqueline du Pré, the unfortunate wife of Daniel Barenboim, the pianist whom I heard play Beethoven's Sonata No. 13 in the Teatro Colón, and cellists (as happened and continues to happen to me, Nora García, and as happened, too, to Jacqueline du Pré when she played) have to hold the violoncello between their legs because when one plays the cello it becomes an obstinate part of one's body, and the body is tuned, tempered as though one were tuning, tempering an instrument. It is a difficult instrument, demanding daily practice—if one doesn't practice every day (as Brailowski said, referring to the piano), first the performer begins to notice and to wince, then the performer's closest friends (if they are musicians, too), and then the public. The body, there is no doubt about it, I repeat, is also an instrument—you're telling *me*?, who has to put the cello between my legs and adapt to it, to the point that I often forget it's an instrument and, without my realizing it, it begins to change (I repeat) into a mere extension of my body? And this principle that applies to the cello applies also to singers, especially if they sing baroque music, that music composed especially for the artificial throat of the castrati (whose larynx did not descend as it does in men because their testicles also did not descend as men's do when their voice changes, for the pure and simple reason that they had been castrated), yes, if one is to perform it (baroque music, if one is a singer—countertenor or castrato) one has to learn how to imitate all the instruments and construct from one's throat and one's entire body another instrument like the others—perhaps the most imprecise, perverse, and delicate of all the instruments that were constructed in the eighteenth century, an instrument which nevertheless was able to give the voice flexibility, power, limpidity, and brilliance. Now, in this age when baroque music has become fashionable once again, countertenors trained especially to replace castrati also construct their voice, as though it were just another instrument, and then they learn to use it as though that were simply an incontrovertible fact, a fait accompli. Children, boys, are more spontaneous, and one can hear that, sense that in their voice when they sing in chorus one of Bach's cantatas conducted by Nikolaus Harnoncourt. The piano is different—one sits on the bench, one's feet planted firmly on the floor, or the tips of one's toes very softly resting on the pedal (sometimes pianists wear very shiny shoes or boots, like those worn by Daniel Barenboim in his concerts) and the sounds are held for a long, long time to give them a velvety tone, yes, the hands rest on the keyboard, the back curves, leans forward, and the face assumes ecstatic expressions—the ecstatic expressions portrayed on the faces of the young performers in a concert painted by Caravaggio, Michelangelo Merisi da Caravaggio—while the cello, on the other hand, I, Nora García say, the cello becomes an integral part of the body, especially the body of women—female cellists place the cello between their legs as though a man were making love to them, which is why novices in convents were forbidden to play it, and the daughters of aristocratic families, too, in the old days—now they aren't, because opening one's legs has become a sign of fashion, and models, even the anorexic ones, are always photographed with their legs spread, as though fashion had usurped what had once been the hallmark of whorehouses. There is a smaller repertoire for the cello, and in general (there are some exceptions—Bach's sonatas for cello, for example) it has to alternate with other instruments, be part of an ensemble, a chamber orchestra, for example, or (in the smallest case) an accompaniment to the piano. Juan played, played the piano, and I play and played the cello and I do not and did not need accompaniment when I play or played pieces for solo cello— for example, Bach's sonatas for cello or Marin Marais's sonatas for viola da gamba. You may be sure that the piano is the most complete of all instruments, that its sonorities are orchestral (although the organ surpasses it, surpasses all other instruments on account of its orchestral capabilities, its tense and enormous range, which is why Bach was, above all, an organist in Leipzig), and perhaps that can be felt, sensed immediately in several of Schubert's sonatas for piano. The piano outshines all other instruments because it is sufficient unto itself, Juan would say, and attempt to demonstrate, although I don't, and didn't, agree—but Juan loved to say, very grandly, that it didn't need an accompanist, which was precisely one of the reasons he devoted himself to the piano. Yes, Juan played the piano and wrote his compositions on music paper and then, when computers came into their own, he learned to transcribe his compositions directly onto the computer keyboard.

A good musical performance demonstrates perhaps the most profound emotional sincerity—the true emotion that is born in the heart, the emotion that an artist is able to transfer to the sounds, an emotion that entails something "personal" but at the same time surpasses it. We know this perfectly well: in the performance of a musical work, the voice of the heart is modulated (the universal voice of the heart), for otherwise the performance would be inane, totally empty, sterile, and perverse. That is why most modern performers prefer the original instruments and voices for which the musical works of the past were composed—many of those instruments, obviously, have disappeared, but some are still perfectly preserved: hunting oboes (the oboe da caccia), natural oboes, recorders, transverse flutes, piston trumpets, bassoons, cornets, timpani, French horns (which the Spanish call English!), violoncellos, violas da gamba, theorbos, lutes, violini-piccoli. These new orchestras use instruments built by craftsmen of the seventeenth and eighteenth centuries to achieve a truer performance, and so it is with the viola signed by Marcellus Holmayer of Vienna (1650) or Andreas Beer's violoncello-piccolo (likewise Vienna, 1685) or Leonardo Stastny's or Gottfried Hechtl's recorders, signed in 1750 by those craftsmen in Dresden, or, finally, Paulhan's oboes da caccia (or d'amore), signed in 1720—instruments used by the members of the orchestra conducted by Nikolaus Harnoncourt when they play Bach's cantatas with the Viennese Boys Choir or the boys choirs of Tölzer or Hannover. It may be impossible, on the other hand, to reproduce the voice of the castrati, and to prove that, a single example should suffice: the early-twentieth-century disc that (badly) reproduces the voice of the last castrato gives us guttural, off-pitch sounds—the wails and shrieks of a cat in heat. But there is one extraordinary case, the recording of a voice that perfectly recreates the most delicate registers of adolescent boys, or of women, and that voice emerges from the throat of David Daniels, the countertenor (almost supernatural is the voice of the dwarf singer with the lovely face, whose mother took thalidomide during her pregnancy).

The heart is the center of life, a human clock, a machine that perfectly measures out our earthly, corporeal time, the flywheel of life which, in a slow arterial concerto, manifests its well-regulated movement. The heart can and should be conceived in many different ways—even as a machine that governs our physiology—that is, as part of an organic corporal mechanism that keeps us alive, and thus as an object of scientific and technical study. It is important to emphasize that in the seventeenth century William Harvey's discoveries regarding the circulation of the blood showed, physiologically, the paths, the routes taken by the blood's flow, and that Descartes, in his Traité des passions de l'âme, already recognized the reciprocal relations between the heart and the brain: he believed that certain passions could produce changes in the blood and express the most profound movements of the heart. In 1625, Sanctorius, a Viennese physician, invented a pulse-meter, the first machine to calculate the frequency of heartbeats (50 or 100 beats per minute), and in the early nineteenth century the Frenchman René Laënnec published a study describing the four successive steps that a good cardiologist should follow: inspection, auscultation, palpation, and percussion. Laënnec later invented the stethoscope, a device that allows one to hear heartbeats and the sounds of breathing. In those long conversations (or rather monologues) we would have in this very place where we are now sitting with his body laid out in state, Juan would tell us that the heart was associated with a particular symbol, a very ancient form of worship, the Sacred Heart of Jesus—a form of worship that gave new significance to ancient religious symbols in order to give singular attention to the corporality and thus humanity of Christ—symbols that recognize the coexistence of parallel discourses between science and religion, which work on each other, and also on poetry. The heart is the center of life, a human clock, a machine that perfectly measures out our earthly, corporeal time, the flywheel of life which, in a slow arterial concerto, manifests its well-regulated movement. Flaubert thought that when women talked about the heart they were actually talking about other parts of the body, and Roland Barthes would say that the word denoted a broad spectrum of movements and desires, often transformed into a gift-object—well or ill received, or even rejected. Is the heart the organ of desire? That is how it's conceived—imprisoned—in the realm of the imaginary (of course, as we know, the heart swells, then relaxes, like one's sex, and in addition, I add, the heart can be broken, split in two or three or four, as happened to Juan). Where shall the movements of the heart end? The pure, sincere movements of the heart? I ask myself that, just now, here, at this very instant, with unhealthy curiosity: What do you suppose the people attending this funeral are feeling?

What am I feeling? What must Juan have felt just before his heart burst into a thousand pieces?

The heart regulates the body but the body, in turn, functions as a shelter and prison for the heart, a jail against love or the onslaughts of fate: the chest as a fortress, or rather as a kind of protective vest (a straitjacket?) so that emotion does not overflow: the heart shattered in your hands. Many poets have employed an arsenal of images of warfare: The flesh undergoes a metamorphosis and becomes mineral (stone), in order to make one safer against the siege of love— often, of course, unsuccessfully. The heart is tempered like steel, and therefore, paradoxically, becomes an object of magnetic attraction: My daughters, Bishop Fernández de Santa Cruz wrote in his will to his favorite nuns, the nuns in the Santa Mónica convent in Puebla, my daughters, the bishop repeats, Juan says, reading aloud from the old book, in this my last will and testament, I order that my heart be taken from my chest, and that it be buried in your choir, and with you, so that it may be in death where it was in life. And for the memory of those that come after you, upon my portrait set this plaque: Daughters, pray to God for this man who gave you his heart. Maybe he should have requested that before he was buried (before Juan was buried) his heart be given to me, so that I could dry it and keep it in a vessel as a relic, a relic that I could have kept beside my bed, mounted in a frame that was also in the shape of a heart (what a perfectly, sublimely kitschy idea!).

Santa Chiara da Montefalco, who took the name Della Croce, of the cross, Juan is saying during one of those long sessions that we would have beside the unlighted fireplace in the other house, those sessions when we would all sit and listen to him, a glass of tequila in our hands (or while I stand near a railing in the yard and listen to María's beautiful voice—that voice that reminds me of the voice of a castrato— telling the story of his death, the death of Juan, that musician who was once my husband), in that living room, I say, we were listening to Juan tell the story of Santa Chiara da Montefalco, who died in the odor of sanctity in 1308 and became the object of a very special operation performed in the interests of modesty by her sisters in the convent, who skillfully—suspiciously skillfully (: an aside by Juan)—sliced open her body and removed from it the viscera, especially the heart, which had grown to disproportionate size, and immediately locked it (the heart) into a box and the next day opened the organ, to see whether its gigantism might be due to some miracle: when one of the nuns opened it, she discovered inside it, perfectly formed, below the nerves, the shape of a cross made flesh, and when she delicately palpated that miraculous heart she found another small nerve which also detached itself from the organ (the heart, the organ of the emotions), and when she looked at it carefully she discovered that it was no less than a representation of the lash that Christ had been flogged with (or at least, Juan explained, that was what the nuns and priests who examined the viscera and gave their verdicts thought)—it was, Juan repeated, it was a replica of the Sacred Heart of Jesus and the instruments of the Passion! Life, that absurd wound.

Bishop Santa Cruz's heart, on the other hand, protected when alive by the pericardial membrane and the walls, the armor of the ribs, was described in the most detailed, almost scientific, way by his contemporaries, those who delivered his eulogy (in the chapel at the cemetery Juan's eulogy is delivered by the man in the long, very well-cared-for moustache who sang a song by José Alfredo Jiménez with the mariachis, as though it were an aria from some opera), and back when we were at home (our house), everyone chatting, with my robust, bossy friend sitting silently by my side in her austere navy blue V-necked sweater and a glass of tequila in her hand and her low-heeled shoes, Juan explains that those analogies had of necessity to point back toward ancient religious symbols. The words spoken during the bishop's funeral services were preserved—forever?—in writing, Juan assures us, and to prove it, he read to us aloud, as though he himself were the prelate who delivered the bishop's eulogy in the church in Puebla: To keep the heart alive for the life of the spirit, nature provides for it in the life of the body, giving to the heart two guards, standing always by it, and these serve the heart not solely as defense and a strong fortress for its preservation (Juan goes on reading to us in his strong, echoing, operatic voice), but also as a form of governor or term to the movement of its vitality. The inward guard, which is called the pericardium, is that tunic or sack of membrane which, filled with aqueous, cooling humor, enshrouds it (like my cello's silk-lined case), with such proportion in the distance that as the heart moves, as it dilates, nothing, noooothing, harms it, and to that end, there is the humor which likewise cools it, and when this humor is lacking, the heart grows fatigued, it is damaged, crippled, crippled—that is, it is lacerated and torn, and this, my sons and daughters, causes a man to plunge into a veritable abyss of pain.

And Juan would interrupt himself for a few moments before going on with the rest of the sermon, his voice intense and tragic (smoking his cigarette and standing up, as though he were delivering a funeral oration, with more solemnity than a simple parish priest officiating at the funeral mass, the exequial high mass of Juan's burial): It is by the abundance of that humor that the heart is preserved, is made joyful, is able to dilate, and this, my sons and daughters, means to bathe in joy. The other guard by which the heart is sheltered is the strong wall of the chest and the palisades of the ribs, and this defense and the other, this guard and the other, stand watch always, to preserve the origin of our life.... Nature has thrown up these walls to defend it. And it is the desire of King Solomon in the Bible that the spiritual, mystical heart, the source and origin of the life of the soul, be protected with the same defenses and the same strong guards as the body's heart is protected by nature. And as those two that I have told you—the membrane of the pericardium and the wall or palisade of the ribs—serve both in life and in allegory as the sepulcher of a living heart, then in death may they serve also as the sepulcher of the dead heart.

The heart of Jesus, Juan explains, is a factory for making blood, and it is managed and supervised by the Eternal Father, who uses the heart's blood as though it were a fuel, a fuel to light the passions: there is a painting that shows a garden watered by a curious hydraulic mechanism, the garden of faith in Christ watered by His blood.

If the heart alone is true and the word is mendacious, what could we do to make our beloved know—see—the truth of our passion? The chest is like a suit of armor that protects the heart and prevents it from being broken. What the heart says, the mouth seems to express, yet that correlation ends in a rhetorical deceit, because words often lie. (Was Juan not unfaithful to me, though he swore eternal love?) (When Rogozhin stabbed Nastashya Filippovna, did he seek perhaps to penetrate the depths of her heart, discover her true emotions, her true affections?): One must go to the other organs of the body to X-ray the heart and love: a shift reveals that: the eyes may replace the mouth (María's torn and rent mouth, that absurd wound); we may not just see, but also hear with our eyes—listen to me with your eyes—, and if the beloved weeps, the tears make up, most forcefully, for ideas, and become the irrefutable proof of mute eloquence. María's disappeared mouth? Can a woman who weeps strip her soul naked? Does weeping allow others a glimpse of the true heart? For the tears that grief pours forth have been distilled by the broken heart, yes, lovers say, I gave you, I gave you my heart, I gave you my heart—you are holding its pieces in your hands!

His heart shattered in their hands, the hands of those who operated on him: Juan is now in the operating room, the surgeons doing open heart surgery on him. Hippocrates and

Galen imposed a taboo that lasted for two thousand years: the heart is sacred: the heart is located inside the chest, protected by the pericardium and the ribs, an inner sanctuary—inviolate, inviolable, impossible to penetrate (or repair): that, at least, was what people thought until 1896: on September 7 of that year, a young gardener named Wilhelm Justus (of the German city of Frankfurt) was stabbed in the chest by three persons unknown (they may have been drinking with him in a tavern), surgeon Jürgen Thorvald tells us, and left for dead in a public park. Three hours later, a police officer patrolling the area found him, in extremis, and had him transported to the central hospital, whose physician on duty at the time was a young man named Siegel. Justus was unconscious, his breathing labored, his face yellow, his nostrils flaring with the labor of respiration, his lips pathetically distorted. Siegel observed that Justus had a stab wound (more than a centimeter wide) near the fourth rib, and he examined the kitchen knife that had made the wound—found some hundred meters from the wounded man! Dr. Ludwig Rehn, a famous surgeon, the hospital's chief medical officer, was not to be back in the hospital until the next day, September 8. Siegel noted that the knife had penetrated the heart, yet the heart was still beating; the man's pulse, however, was very weak. He picked up a probe and introduced it into the chest to calculate the damage, which was obviously considerable. Siegel was sure that Justus was going to die at any moment; his heart was beating weakly, 50 beats per minute. The police officer who had brought him in would not leave him, and he asked whether there was any hope. Siegel shook his head, remembering at that instant an observation made by one of Germany's most renowned surgeons: A surgeon who dares to penetrate the heart shall immediately lose the esteem of his colleagues, and well deserves to. Siegel was not an exceptional doctor, but he did see that the wound was small and that internal hemorrhaging would slowly yet surely kill the patient; he also undoubtedly remembered that several centuries earlier, Hippocrates and Galen had predicted that wounds to the heart would lead inevitably to death.

Siegel ordered that the patient be given camphor and that ice be put on the wound. The police officer was unmoving, although he did ask (with some hesitation) whether Dr. Rehn would be coming back soon. Siegel was offended—did the officer doubt his skill as a physician? He was certain the patient would be dead by the time Rehn came into the ward the next day.

But he was not.

Rehn examined Justus: his face, now marked by death, almost lifeless, his pulse thin and thready, his wrist moist with sweat, his breathing superficial and labored, his lungs severely compromised by the internal hemorrhage—and yet the external wound to the heart was no longer bleeding, and the heart was beating weakly. Rehn quickly took in the situation: the knife had penetrated the pericardium, its point had touched the wall (perhaps but barely scratching or nicking it), but any wound of this type caused a slow escape of blood, and the blood would slowly fill the heart until it stopped it, due to inexorably increasing pressure—as had happened to Nastasya Filippovna. The wound may have been large enough to allow the blood to leak into the thoracic cavity (the thoracic cavity expands in a very particular way in young boys who have been castrated, which allows the voice to expand and reach registers of great intensity). Yes, Rehn told himself, the fatal compression of the heart has not occurred and Justus has a slight possibility of survival. The heart will go on working until the last drop of blood has been squeezed out of it, and then the blood will invade the lungs and exert such pressure on them that the sick man will stop breathing (Had the same thing happened to Nastasya Filippovna?). I'll try to do something, he told himself—either way, he's a dead man. Do you suppose he thought, before doing it, about some of the previous attempts to penetrate that (so far) inviolable sanctuary?, the case of a man who attempted to kill himself by stabbing himself in the heart, in the times of Napoleon, and whom the famed surgeon Larrey tried (unsuccessfully) to save, by opening the patient's chest (with no anesthesia whatsoever) and touching, for the first time!, with his finger, the apex of the heart? Or the case of an English boilermaker who was operated on (successfully) in 1872 by English surgeon George Callender, who extracted a needle that had lodged in his heart during a whorehouse brawl? Had not Callender made a tiny incision in the chest, removed the needle, and sutured the heart as he followed the rhythms of systole and diastole?

But never before had a surgeon dared to entirely open the chest of a man and handle the very heart itself! He must have shuddered suddenly, felt a sudden wave of nausea—do you suppose his blood pressure rose, his pulse accelerated (150 or 200 beats a minute?)?: what would he feel when he opened the chest, violated it, penetrated the sanctuary for the first time and held—at last!—a heart in his hands?, totally exposed it, contemplated its functioning, made an incision (or two), stanched the wound, introduced a needle, sutured the wound, closed the chest again, waited for the sternum to fuse?, how can one take in one's hands a living, palpitating heart? (human sacrifice?), how can one push a needle through a muscle in constant movement?, how to take advantage of its rhythm?, its well-regulated movement?, its arterial concerto? But it was not enough to imagine this—he had to make the decision, the decision to break through the prison, take the heart (the shattered, broken heart) in his own hands.

Justus was still alive, though very weak now, but he withstood the anaesthesia. Rehn made a long incision in the sternum—how much work to break through the bone! (the bone dust flying), and as he did so he could hear much more clearly the beating of the heart; he made a second incision, near the fifth rib; the thorax was full of coagulated blood; he pushed one of his fingers inside (the second, the longest, the finger that Renaissance philosophers believed was connected to the heart?), and he felt that he was touching the pericardium. He cut through the pleura, and much more blood gushed out (his assistants could hardly stop it) and the lung collapsed. Could the heart withstand this? The pericardium appeared, and he saw the damage that the knife had done to the muscle. He tried to clamp it, so he could work, open the incision a bit, go in deeper. Several times he had to repeat the process because the skin of the pericardium would tear and blood gush out. At last he managed to pull the pericardium back and reach the heart: there it was, beating irregularly in its constant expansion (diastole) and contraction (systole); he was able to determine the type of wound the knife had produced—in the exact center of the right ventricle, it measured about a centimeter long, and blood was coming from it in little drops. Instinctively, Rehn put his finger on it: immediately, the wound stopped bleeding. His finger slipped away when the heart contracted; when it expanded again, he would touch the wound again, and he tried to close it with a thin needle and a silk suture, his hands moving with the continual alternating expansion and contraction that keeps the heart alive. With the diastole, the wound was exposed, and with an agile movement he took the first stitch in the left side of the wound, then waited a brief instant (a century!) for the heart to resume its rhythm before taking the second stitch and suturing, fearing always that the heart would cease to beat. When he finished the suturing, the wound had stopped bleeding and the pulse became stronger. He cleaned the pericardium and the thorax of its clotted blood, replaced the rib, and closed the outer wound. Two hours later, Justus was breathing easily.

If one is not careful when one arrives in La Paz, Bolivia, one can die instantly of a heart attack, and to avoid that one has to wait, calmly, for about three days, until the number of red corpuscles increases and the blood is oxygenated again, to return to the ordinary rhythm of one's life. A famous German orchestra conductor died almost the minute he got off the plane at Los Altos Airport, which lies some 4,000 meters above sea level: a massive heart attack ended his long, successful career.

If I'm not mistaken, it was not until 1948 that surgeons once more dared to open a patient's chest and dilate one of the heart valves. Open heart operations became routine about ten years later, and since 1970, progress in this area has been astounding. The patient must be put into a temporary non-physiological state, because the organism cannot stand to have its circulation halted for more than three minutes. In the beginning, other procedures were used: hypothermia (lowering the body temperature to 28 degrees Centigrade, about 82 degrees Fahrenheit) and hyperbaria, which consisted in increasing the oxygen pressure in the blood. Today, artificial organs are used, an artificial heart and artificial lungs, so that the brain can continue to receive its essential blood supply.

The limpidness of the language in which men and women have written sentimental poetry, the poetry of the heart, coincides with the quality of tears—their transparency—; indeed, the impenetrable armor which isolates the inner organ, hidden within the thorax, covered by muscles and skin, could also be pierced, long before open heart surgery existed, by the simple force of love, love which operates by a kind of alchemical transmutation whose product is that precipitate of love, the liquid humor which through an exaltation of the passions is the clear, faithful, though metaphorical, proof of a faithful, loving heart, undone (shattered, broken) by love (and love of truth). To operate on Juan, the doctors cover their hands with thin latex gloves; their instruments are stained with blood, a humor much thicker than that produced by the eyes—those tears which, unlike the blood, are transparent. Tears make it possible for the lover to see the transition between the invisible and the visible: emotions which seem false when expressed only with words and concrete actions—caresses, for example, or gifts—are pale reflections of its veracity, the veracity of the heart (the truth of the heart), and the only sincere and necessary tears we shed are those that wet the hands of the beloved, like the tears that I once shed on Juan's hands when he put them to my face—those tears, the irrefutable proof of my truest and most intense emotion. Is only a vulgar heating of the blood, an alchemical operation, capable of reiterating the miracle of requited love?

Certain modifications of the blood cause movements in the countenance, such as happiness or despair: the blood is warmed, becomes rarefied, convulses—can the blood convulse?, or is it the heart that convulses? Yes, the passion of love sets physiological mechanisms in motion, yes, under the influence of passion the blood is warmed and a kind of effervescence is created which pushes the blood as it leaves the heart, yes, life, that absurd wound! And that is literally what happens when one is struck (wounded) by love—its fire shatters the heart, the organ of life (my heart is shattered in your hands), and that extreme emotion allows the blood to boil. It's true, absolutely true, the blood boils and its fire creates a combustion, as though we set a pot of water on it, and when the water boils it evaporates, the process of heating effects a poetic movement: the transmutation of words into tears causes the blood to distill and vaporize into ardors through the eyes. By grace of the metaphor of love, the heart appears to be distilled like liquor, although actually, if one is alive, the armor of the chest remains intact and tears are but the expression—the reflection—of requited love. A unique formula exists for breaking the heart, metaphorically broken into pieces by passion or turned to transparent liquid that serves as a mirror. That possibility might be expressed by saying that certain ways of dying make death liquid—that is, turn death into duration and purification. To cause the heart to break, to split in two, not metaphorically but literally, an open heart operation is required, so that the chest may gush forth blood and the lustful flame be extinguished. When the thorax is actually opened, when that strongbox that protects the heart—formed by the sternum and the ribs—is broken through, when the chest is violently split open, death results, as the death of Juan resulted, or the death of Nastasya Filippovna, who might have been saved had someone performed open heart surgery on her, like that operation performed for the first time on a patient by the German surgeon Rehn in 1896.

In her convulsive talking, María has spoken the word death, Juan's death, and blood seems to gush from her mouth, altering nature, turning it all to red. Death is perhaps the most violent form of requited love, if from the two interlinked chests blood gushes. It is the blood of Juan that has been spilled. I hear my heart beating, my blood flowing, slowly, and as rhythmically as a metronome (from 50 to 100 beats a minutes), within my own heart, while I sit beside the body of Juan. And so the two chains of metaphors are intertwined, the metaphor of the heart and the metaphor of tears, the metaphor of the heart and the metaphor of blood—two ways of producing wetness, two ways of breaking the heart, the only two ways the prison can be destroyed, that prison of bones and flesh. In murder, in suicide (in cases of murder or suicide, the chest has been penetrated violently and the heart has been exposed) and also in an operation (to replace the natural arteries with plastic ones, or to replace the tissues of the mitral valve with a pig or cow valve), the chest is split open and the heart exposed to view—in fact, the doctors can hold it in their hands, Juan's shattered heart in their hands. Yes, Sor Juana says, for I, more sensible in my fortune, have in my two hands two eyes, and only what I touch do see.

Olive oil, María explains, interrupting her story (her mouth shines), contains 77 percent monosaturated fat, the good fat (HDL), the fat that helps reduce bad cholesterol

(LDL). Researchers believe that olive oil, María repeats (and she does so with her tiny mouth, her lips pursed in anger), may reduce the risk of heart disease and some types of cancer, not to mention that it helps keep blood pressure stable and gives some relief from arthritis. Easily digestible, she adds, olive oil may reduce stomach acid, heal ulcers, and stimulate the liver, intestine, and pancreas (like avocado, maybe, too). If your blood pressure is not high, she adds, you don't have to worry too much, even if your cholesterol is high—at our age, cholesterol doesn't mean a thing, although, she says, speaking even louder (and causing everyone around us to turn around and listen), you do have to keep your blood pressure down (but I know what she says isn't true— cholesterol is bad, you have to eat correctly to lower it, and take Lipitor or Zokor or Mevacor, even if they destroy your liver (and to prevent liver complications, you have to have periodic checkups, at least once every six months)).

I, in turn, allow myself a brief poetic fantasy, allow myself to trace a line between the heart, that essential organ in the shape of a hieroglyphic, the organ of the emotions— the physiology of love?—and the shape of the sonnet. Like the heart, the sonnet is closed upon itself, can never move outside its enclosure, and like the vapor that passion causes to rise and emerge through the eyes, I believe it is due to the effects of combustion—a mere contemptible thermal combination—that the heart can shatter, break, dissolve into tears—be destroyed. The form of the sonnet is very much like the heart's, this delicate instrument closed in upon itself which, overflowing, occasions the death of the body—in this particular case, the death of Juan's body—and also the death of the poem.

Beginning and end are joined, as in the esoteric symbol of the Ouroboros, the serpent that bites its own tail, the perfect allegory of the Infinite, and also of the Eternal Return (: as though one were to say wrestling with the angel). The town is lovely—set in the mountains like a pale blue jewel, its cobbled streets rising and falling, leading to the dusty town square, the plaza. Nothing seems to have changed since the last time I was here, although Juan's death changes things, as it has changed his house, our house: now it rains less, perhaps, and one notes much more clearly the ashen color of the earth—like the ashen color of his face and the prickliness of the moustache that disfigures him? In the fields I have seen sheaves of dry straw—piled, stubborn, misshapen, misformed, tousled, clumsily placed here and there, as though they were hungry and thirsty, set out in the open and exposed to wind and rain, so different from those nature morts that Juan and I admired in European museums, the Dutch and Spanish still-lifes—the Spaniards with their fruits and insects, the Dutch with their fields illuminated by the sun shining on the haystacks, illuminating them as though from inside, haystacks that will be used to feed the animals, fill the granaries, haystacks the countrypeople cut and gather or bale, and the yellow straw of the fields is stacked to form perfectly triangular pyramids, in perfect equilibrium, and they are painted with great technical skill and spiritual fragility, haystacks, sheaves crowned with knots that rivet them in silence, the silence of an autumnal peace. In other paintings the countryfolk are sitting in groups, eating, the children playing, the men drinking, some of them cutting a big loaf of bread, a woman fixing her hair under her bonnet; behind them, the stacks of hay are triumphant structures whose stubborn surfaces speak of abundance—I begin on one side of the canvas and end on the other, go over the painting, take an inventory of the objects that appear in it, and to me, what most stands out is the way the gleaming stacks of yellow hay deliver themselves up so passively, so sweetly—that autumnal peace that Gould wanted to achieve when he performed, shortly before he died, Johann Sebastian Bach's Goldberg Variations.

Along the roads of Mexico, as I drive toward the town to add my name to the list of mourners, those attending a wake and a funeral for the dead, the stacks of dry straw fill me with melancholy—in their worn, tattered, sloppily-laid-out appearance, I see the fragile shadow of loss, I think, as I drive down the town's main street, which is also a rural highway, with its improvised stands displaying greens, peas, beans, tied bunches of orange carrots, slabs of meat, orange and green chorizos (the droning buzz of flies), the ringing of the church bells echoing sadly in my heart. In Dutch paintings, the laboriousness, the hardness of the work is balanced by a green band that speaks to us of a fertile earth almost idyllic in its glorification of everyday values—the hay the memory of an abundant harvest, usable down to the last straw, the last bit of chaff, proud in its efficiency.

I am still standing near the coffin, and I stare almost unblinkingly at the yellowish face with its new, unfortunate moustache, which occupies the place of the teeth, the straw-colored face with its jaw tied so it won't fall open, this anonymous face, the absence of gaze. Mythification—is this a memory?—shapes a story, engenders new, fleeting bodies, but the word always corrects them, slowly transforms them, polishes their features, their face, Juan's face, the face of the Juan that I carry in my memory, the Juan I spent so many years with, whose now deathly-pale face reminds me of the color of hay stacked in the fields (those happy fields of memory and of Dutch paintings that the two of us stood before in those early days when we still held hands), it turns into the face of a person whom the years have touched, an endless movement seems imprinted on every line, the model dissolves, and a different trace is sketched—will it replace the face and countenance of memory, will the last one be this one that I am now contemplating for the last time?

It's not him anymore, I'm not me, we have stopped being us, we are other, as though one had departed oneself, from the back, from the eyes, from the belly, from the chest...I look at him again, with curiosity, I recall his effusions of affection, the effusions of years ago, and I wonder, as I did then, where does he want to go with this? Or rather, where did he want to go? Effusions that tore one from one's own body, organ by organ, particle by particle, that opened one, multiplied one: I remember that curiosity would sometimes (sometimes, not always) make me keep my eyes open, that a desperate eagerness to know would leave the pleasure incomplete—I wanted to know, always to know where we might finally get to—and then suddenly, clouding everything, pleasure—a total pleasure that was sometimes followed by nausea, or disgust (aren't they the same thing?), a terrible disgust, a rejection, no more embraces, no more kisses or sighs or promises, a few tears as thick as sperm, a soft, supple caress, tender yet slimy, suffocating—sordid? A heart sullied by none-too-virtuous intentions, a heart injured by so much misery.

Is that the way the funeral is going to be? I ask myself, interrupting the memory, stabilizing my body, softening the nausea: light, tender, supple, and at the same time slimy, suffocating—sordid? How is one to describe sordidness? Should I explain it by simply repeating the word sordid? Everything mixes together—sordidness, tenderness, and at the same time the absurdity of it all (this is almost a parody of a funeral), the flies, the dung, the pebbles, the huaraches, the dirty feet, as though every leg were a hoof, the drunk beggar with his bandaged foot, and on the bandage fresh bloodstains, and along the road the prints of ox and cow hooves, horseshoes. On the beggar's face, effort, every step he takes is painful—we have to climb the hill, there's dust, and pebbles, and also cow dung—his step is pitiful yet obscene, and his coarse, knowing gaze becomes a gross gesture that accompanies the body, the body of a shrunken man, all that's left of him is a dried-out skin, yellowish, the color of haystacks that dot the countryside all along the highway, ill-tied bales, straggly-haired, misshapen, mean-spirited-looking bales, similar in their degradation and decay to the countryside itself, which has gradually decayed due to lack of rain, due to the wholesale razing of the forests—the earth sterile, yellow, shriveled. A man whose heart once beat rhythmically (50 to 100 beats a minute) but has stopped working: a heart wounded by death. Do you think anyone will finally notice that it's me, Nora García, that they should give their most heartfelt condolences to?

I take the subway, the red line, to the Museum of Fine Arts in Boston. Across from me, an ad: Do you have diabetes and take insulin? Take care of your heart. Obviously, mine is beating fast, more than 100 beats a minute. The ticket costs $12, since I'm a senior citizen. If I were a regular person it would have cost $16: I am consoled to learn that I can come back to the museum whenever I want for a month. It is a huge museum, very modern, full of flags—little ones, big ones—American flags, multicolored statues flying through the air—they are young, elastic, healthy athletes, their hearts very healthy, several galleries with installations and paintings that I wander through almost without stopping; the exceptions are a few paintings, a handful of statues, certain photographs (they are almost always exhibited in the hallways, as though museums weren't sure where to put them: art or document?). I enter a dimly-lit room where a reproduction of the last Japanese temple constructed in the eighth century has been installed—the temple brought over intact from Japan by illustrious Bostonians who bought it before it was torn down; it is the oratory reserved for the priests, and it is now devoid of worshippers, visited only by a few curious souls who examine its wooden walls, the lamps, the Buddhas.

The next gallery contains miniatures, jade perfume-bottles with coral tops, or cinnabar with venturine (or ivory with amethyst), I examine them closely, I grow bored, I walk through other rooms, enormous rooms, a succession of display cases with amphorae, hydrias, urns, Greek kraters and Egyptian sarcophaguses and necklaces and combs, and boxes and cats, and enormous rigid statues with sophisticated, incredibly complex hair styles and one foot forward, all perfectly preserved, as though all of them had just been made, objects identical to those in the Metropolitan Museum of New York, and the Louvre, and the British Museum, and the Pergamon in Berlin—as though the lands of Egypt or Greece or Rome or Mexico had produced thousands and thousands of little figures, vessels, tombs, statues, so that the museums of the world might be decorated with them, with enough left over to adorn the less elegant, less privileged museums in their own countries of origin. How fortunate! I think, how fortunate that millionaires become so obsessed with some specific kind of object that they collect them and house them in their palaces and then, when they die, leave them to museums so that one of the museum's galleries can display a plaque with the millionaire's name, like a gravestone! I prefer Lila Acheson, however: the enormous niches in the lobby of the Metropolitan Museum where immense flower arrangements are displayed, in perpetual homage to her memory.

I make a quick association while I wander through the vast galleries of Marshall Field's in Chicago (located on the Miracle Mile)—a building of several stories all opening onto the first where, perfectly categorized, every sort of item imaginable is on display: famous designer dresses, sweaters, raincoats, towels, pots and pans, cosmetics, boys' and girls' clothing, bathing suits, carpets, objects laid out elegantly to attract consumers. The day I visited, however, there were none—I was completely alone in the store, which had that still, funereal air (the air of an old-fashioned funeral or a New England burial ground, ascetic and aseptic) that one finds in the large museum galleries that house the permanent collection when one of the big blockbuster temporary exhibitions is on display—those shows full of people because they've just opened, and they've been advertised and reviewed in newspapers and magazines, and one can penetrate their deepest meanings if one rents headphones with recordings in all the official languages, and finally, when one leaves the exhibition, one can purchase posters, postcards, catalogues, jewelry reproductions, necklaces, bookbags, scarves, ties, sweatshirts as a souvenir of the experience.

On the radio and in the papers, a breaking story: in a crematory in the state of Georgia, in the United States, uncremated bodies have been found dating back more than twenty years, some in a state of complete decomposition: their loved ones had received urns with "ashes" that were actually concrete dust, wood shavings, and dirt. Abuse of the elderly, violence, and even rape is reported in nursing homes. Priests continue to sexually abuse the boys in their parishes. In the near future, atomic bombs will be used once more to combat evil.

For some reason I cannot quite understand, as I write these lines describing Juan's funeral I am reading Sebald or Dostoevsky, Bernhard or Rousseau, and I am listening to Seppi Kronwitter sing, the Tölzer boy singer on the recording of the Bach cantata that Nikolaus Harnoncourt conducted (a boy eternally young thanks to this recording, or rather a voice preserved in its perfect, angelic childhood by the magic of recording), some of the characters are seated, him, them, me. After we divorced, Juan lived for a while in a modest house in town and got around on an old bicycle. But in my text he is listening, like me, and he too is writing, to Rameau's Pygmalion. He is listening to it while he writes (in longhand) in his diaries or transcribes notes onto stave-lined paper (Jean-Jacques Rousseau's principal occupation, by which he earned a living) and the sound emerges from a simple radio-cassette player combination, while I listen to it on a traditional record player and am sitting in my red armchair writing on a typewriter. The table is big, crude, green from use and kitchen acids—olive oil—that have stained it irremediably, forever (or as long as it lasts). At this very moment the record gets stuck (I wish I had Juan's cassette player—besides, mine only plays acetate, "wax," it's totally archaic, we're in the DVD age now), the ambiguous voice of the countertenor endlessly repeating l'amour, l'amour, l'amour, l'amour, words that I repeat too, and that Juan repeated in his choral works and, with admirable constancy, in his diaries. Juan is writing his papers and I, mine. And thus Juan and I are sitting, talking. He, in the photograph, I, in my house, at the table, sitting on a black velvet cushion that goes beyond any bounds of kitsch with its needlepoint flowers, which match the explosive, malignant red of the chair—together, kitsch redundant. Bright, soft, the pincushion of red silk (like a tango?, or a chocolate cherry with brandy liquor filling?). Juan is unhappy, or at least that's what I'd like to think. One day he left his wife (me, Nora García) and children and began to live a wild, voracious life, but that doesn't matter—now, in my text, he is sitting in his chair at a table on which he is writing in his diary, with his perfect handwriting and his gold fountain pen (obsolete, too, like the act of writing in longhand), writing something, I can just make out a phrase or two. Pygmalion is singing or declaiming impassioned words, he is loving, loving, with delirium, as people love only in novels or in operas, his voice accompanies (sometimes patiently, sometimes out of key) the delicate scratching of the pen, which leaves indelible lines on the white page. Juan has lived the unbridled life (what exactly do I mean by that?), but now he is writing (or so, jealous, I wish) and his writing reduces him to a strange passivity, the passivity of sitting monotonously at a table (Rogozhin waited, patiently sitting beside the dead body of Nastasya Filippovna, for the arrival of Prince Myshkin, but instead of candles, four open bottles of Zhdanov liquid were stationed around her), picking up a pen (there are those who prefer pencil), placing it between the thumb and middle finger, the index on top, or placing the tips of the fingers (all but the thumb; did Juan type with all his fingers or just with the index finger of each hand?), placing the tips of the fingers on the keys of a Remington typewriter, or an Olympia, or an even faster, electric one (faster? really?—because when you type you follow your usual rhythm, no matter whether it's on the manual or the electric, although writing by hand is slower, that much is true). One writes as though one had actually lived (Casanova is the best example; he wrote letters to his patrons or love letters to his lovers, and he wrote his memoirs when life—that absurd wound—prevented him, now old and sick, from living as he wanted—he didn't make it to sixty, and yet he couldn't stretch it out for any more—during those years, I say, the last years of his life when he was writing his memoirs, while he was employed as a librarian in Count Waldstein's library at Dux Castle). Or maybe life splits in two and one way of life is fulfilling that strange desire to be immobile—like Juan now, lying in his coffin, and me, sitting next to the casket, staring at him? Or maybe I'm somewhere else, sitting on a black velvet needlepoint cushion at a crude, rustic, old kitchen table (whose smoothness and age are interrupted by an absurd heart-shaped red silk pincushion). (I close my eyes, I see him now, lying before me, almost naked, on a table, his body bristling with needles, in his chest, in his belly and groin, in his ears, above his eyebrows, his forehead sad thinking about life, and in the skin of his neck, near the jugular, an intense wound, the absurd wound that is life: everything is so fleeting!: your heart is made of glass!) When I write, my hands move very differently than Juan's did when he played the piano or mine when I play the cello, because I played, and still in fact play, the cello. To make music with the cello and other stringed instruments you take the bow and place it on the strings, and your right hand moves skillfully, delicately, in order to make a somber, melancholy tone, similar to a lament, which one could hear especially when Jacqueline de Pré, already ill, exerted pressure with her index and middle fingers on the strings and brought forth from her instrument the highest and most moving sounds (though now slightly imperfect). Here, on the other hand, I am typing, and the tapping of my fingers on the machine is monotonous, mediocre, bureaucratic, very different from the intense sound produced by stringed instruments. A marvelous passivity forces us to stop living in order to write, thinking that we're living. On the record, Pygmalion sounds proud, and we know that because the lushness of his voice parallels and intertwines with the bright metallic tones of the trumpets—a sharp sound that vibrates in the closed space of theaters or pierces the open air when it calls men to the hunt (in Telemann's sonatas for trumpet, for example), a sound that is reproduced in the recording that once, truly and concretely, a group of performers performed—is it like the voice of María when I run into her in the yard and she starts telling me, once again, all the details of Juan's death, while her red-painted mouth disappears, leaving just a darker line outlining lips pursed in anger or that remind me of a heart-shaped red silk pincushion I have on my kitchen table?

And all the devotion and all the misery and grief and all the bodies and all the pleasures are concentrated in this hand running swiftly over the page on which, little by little, a text is being written in perfect letters (14 point Arial, Hewlett Packard, gold Mont Blanc fountain pen, broad nib), an attempt to stop life, preserve the memory of a life (l'amour, sings Pygmalion, l'amour toujours, and María insists that his heart broke), that obscure wound that is life. Here Rameau touches me, and the same countertenor (David Daniels photographed: a broad, pear-shaped face, hair—a lot of it— falling over his forehead, bringing out his thick eyebrows and thin moustache, actually more like fuzz covering his upper lip, his chin and jaw also covered with an incipient beard), the same countertenor, I repeat, David Daniels, is singing a melancholy aria (it's not Rameau anymore, it's Händel, but the soprano-like voice of the well-trained falsetto is thrilling, impassioned, as it sings of sadness, disillusion, abandonment), is singing as the castrati once sang, with a voice different from men's because of its lightness, its flexibility, and its sharp sound, and different from the voice of women because of its brilliance, its limpidity, and its power, and superior to the voice of boys because of its perfect adult muscularization, its technique, and its expressivity—and yet those sharp sounds do come very close to those sung by sopranos or those of the boy singers that perform on the record of the Bach cantata (the voice of the boy soprano Seppi Kronwitter conducted by Nikolaus Harnoncourt), because in the anguished modulations of the countertenors there will suddenly slip through the voice of a man in falsetto. One day I discovered a voice that wrenched my heart, the voice of Seppi, young Seppi Kronwitter. I discovered it one day when I was listening to the cantatas recorded by Nikolaus Harnoncourt and Gustav Leonhardt, and on one of them he is the lead singer of the Tölzer Boys Choir. The first time I heard the voice, my pulse raced, and, as the saying goes, my heart was broken. The passage that held me in suspense (for only a few minutes, two maybe) is replaced by another of the soloists, Peter Jelosits, who sings much better, he is much more in tune, his voice is more complete, like the voice of professional sopranos, but the voice of Seppi quivers like the voice of a bird one holds in one's hands to help it escape from a closed room that it entered by mistake (as happens often in my greenhouse), he runs out of breath, and when he tries to reach the highest notes his voice cracks and suddenly, as quickly as it came, disappears. I run the compact disc back a bit and repeat the passage that has so moved me (a true orgasm of the soul) (several times), but his voice has turned into just another voice, a marvelous, well-timbred voice, but just another voice. I try again (it's useless), and I stop listening to the cantatas for a long time. Several months pass, I've forgotten which cantata it was, and the ones I listen to thrill me with their beauty, the extraordinary skill of the composition, and the satisfactory (coherent) performance of a musical work (and, of course, the enormous grandeur of Bach's music). I continue my detective work, which is not to find a perfect voice but rather to rediscover the voice that moved me so deeply before, a voice that has led me to go in search of CDs, which I've lost and keep stubbornly searching for. I do it systematically, I listen (on the record player), one by one, in ascending order, to the Bach cantatas performed by Harnoncourt and Gustav Leonhardt, when at last I come to Cantata No. 53, and the miracle occurs again: I hear the voice, it's the voice of Seppi Kronwitter, a voice between childhood and adolescence, a natural voice that lasts only a second, the second in which the boy is no longer a boy but rather begins to live a life of maturity, that crucial moment when both the larynx and the testicles descend. It is the ephemeral, high, piercing, transparent, unstable (unless, when the boys are six or seven, an operation is performed to preserve the larynx's position, the shape and plasticity of childhood) (the castrati grew enormous, and were a beautiful mixture of man-child-woman that made them irresistible (they awoke perverse desires in the spectators, although to defend themselves from those sentiments, some would insult their patrons, or mock them)): the voice of Seppi is (or was) natural, the voice of an adolescent, an intermediate voice, before the change, because adolescents' voices change.

At the movie theater, I am watching a silent film (Fritz Lang's Metropolis?), and Juan puts his arm around my shoulders (I am eating chocolate-covered raisins, Juan, popcorn), a man is playing the piano. It's Satie's Three Pear-Shaped Pieces, a work that Juan also performs in the huge living room on the Bösendorfer, which is better for playing Schubert on than the Steinway or the Petrof. No, now it's not Satie anymore, it's Händel again, transcribed for the piano. Daniels is suffering and his voice calls out for Cleopatra, the only woman he has ever loved, and the actor, as protean as any good actor (another countertenor) sings a sacred song and life becomes eternal, under the aegis of greasepaint and an undulating song (serpentine column). And thus I, Nora García, sitting at the typewriter, wearing a very full gray skirt (or at the computer) or opening my legs clad in black pants as I play the violoncello, while he, Juan, motionless in memory, constantly writes in his diary with his Mont Blanc fountain pen (it is music paper, he is in his (modest) country house, before he moved here where we are now sitting around the casket, around the body, in the immense studio where there is a piano (a Bösendorfer, a Steinway, or a Petrof?) and several other musical instruments: a cello, flutes, violin (Amati, Stradivarius), scores, books, paintings, flowers, candles) (and a persistent sickly-sweet smell of clotted blood); he has retired for a while to write his books (the result of his research) and his compositions for piano (he writes directly on the staves of the music paper, the computer doesn't exist for that yet), and thus preserved is that space and that time when we would talk, me sitting at my green kitchen table that still preserves the traces of so many substances (a primitive alchemy) (my desk, on which there sits, now uselessly, a red silk pincushion with five pins stuck into it like the acupuncture needles once stuck in Juan's body) and the tips of my fingers would touch the keys of the typewriter as I listened to Rameau's Pygmalion performed by David Daniels and he, Juan, with his heavy gold fountain pen (a Mont Blanc) would be telling the story of his life, writing it in his diaries in ink that reminded me of the color of the Emmanuel Kahn suit being worn at this very instant by María, that brilliant, diabolical, and very perfumed woman who, when she accompanies me along the rocky path that leads up to the cemetery, tells me, untiringly, despite the climb, stories of Juan's death, that's life, she repeats, that's the way it is, a bitch, as your mother used to say, life's a bitch but it's life, you know that, life is an absurd wound. And in her gramophone voice she adds: today's woman doesn't need a man anymore to surround her with luxury, nor do men need women to cover their homosexuality. The tango is like that: an ordering principle of pleasure and at the same time a discourse, more nostalgic than melancholic and more visceral than narcissistic. To suffer, you don't need another person. The melancholy man, and only the bad tango-writer is melancholy, swallows other people and spits out their bones.

Bach's Cantata No. 52 is performed by a chorus, the orchestra, and a soloist (a soprano voice), in this case the boy singer Seppi Kronwitter conducted by Nikolaus Harnoncourt. This composition was written by Bach on November 24, 1726, a year in which he was still writing a cantata a week. The text is based on the Gospels. The structure of the work has a surprising simplicity and clarity: the treachery of the world and the goodness of God are sung, respectively, in a recitative and an aria, after being introduced by an instrumental sinfonia. The work concludes with a chorale in F major whose reference key is D minor. It represents the world of treachery in F minor, and the kingdom of heaven in B flat. The melody is simple despite the excess coloration of the instrumentation—due, perhaps, to the use in the sinfonia of the first movement of the first Brandenburg Concerto (without the piccolo violin). The brilliant sonorities of the sinfonia contrast with the asceticism of the first melody (with its two violins and the basso continuo played on the harpsichord). The true Christian rejects the falseness of the world and scorns it with imprecations, says the priest in the mass for Juan. The virulence of the rejection, declaimed in the first recitative, is juxtaposed against the sweetness of the aria titled Gott ist getreu, repeated several times. The second melody is illuminated by the constant presence of three oboes; its dancelike nature (it is almost a polonaise) praises the grandeur of the divine world and the dance of the soul which is the dance of the true Christian. At the conclusion of the chorale, the full orchestra picks up the theme again, which is marked by the first trumpet and reinforced by the heart-wrenching singing of the boy soprano Seppi Kronwitter, who in this recording (made in 1970) was fifteen years old and is now (perhaps) forty-seven. His boyish voice was remarkable, metallic, nasal, fragile, very thin, almost transparent; the voice of young singer Peter Jelosits (another boy soprano), who accompanies Seppi in Cantata BMV 58, also conducted by Harnoncourt, is fuller, more in tune, more professional, but Seppi's voice, tender, modulated, is moving, it breaks like the voice of a little bird fluttering against the windows of the country house's enormous living room. A performance of Bach's cantatas is genuine only if it is performed by boy singers in the chorus, Harnoncourt believes, in imitation of Bach, who composed for the boys choir of the Church of St. Thomas in Leipzig that he himself directed—a choir his own sons Philip Emmanuel and Johann Christian sang in when they were adolescents. Harnoncourt prefers to use boy singers and period instruments, to give authenticity to his performance, although one can (also) hear in his recordings the voices of famous countertenors, sopranos, basses, and baritones (as I said, Juan repeats, the last time Gould performed the Goldberg Variations was in the broadcast he himself titled To Each Man His Bach).

I am walking beside the beggar, I see the fresh blood (Juan's blood has stopped circulating), in the coffin the body is still wearing the same clothes, the clothes he has been dressed in for the last time, that casual, informal, even banal clothing (à l'anglaise? the careless well-cared-for English country look?) whose desiccated, melancholy color is brought out by the sad tie and the black kerchief that binds his toothless jaws together. I see the beggar's fresh blood, it stains the bandages on his injured foot. In his dusty huaraches he treads the dust of the road. The smell of mold, of mildew haunts me, climbs with me, accompanies me. The imposing fat man, the one who pronounces his words as though he were playing a trombone (his name is Eduardo), the one who was next to the thin woman without a trace of makeup (although she was well dressed), the woman that smiles mechanically each time he pronounces his pompous words. Eduardo, yes, Eduardo is asking, he too is asking to help with the weight of the coffin, to carry it with the others, at the precise moment the relief is being organized, when it's time to replace those who have been carrying it—men, always men, those men carrying it along the rocky path that drops and then climbs again toward the cemetery, the path surrounded by mountains, at that very moment, I say, Eduardo approaches, he leaves the thin woman behind (who do you suppose she is?, his new wife?), approaches, bends down, places the casket on his shoulder, and simultaneously, necessarily lifts it in the air, above all the others: impossible: Eduardo is so huge, so much taller than all the other men, that they can't hold the casket, it's not possible to share the weight, the coffin begins to wobble, to sway: Eduardo is breathing hard, panting, he turns livid, he sweats. A poor man, a humble man in shirtsleeves, his shoes covered in dust and his pants old and worn, rushes over, takes Eduardo's place, sets on his shoulder the rough-hewn pine box with gold-metal fittings, and the procession continues its ascent and descent along the path paved with cow dung, dust, and pebbles.

The path is long, very long, the coffin rocks like a crib on the shoulders of the men carrying it through the rocks, through the pebbles and the songs of the mariachis, the mescal, the tequila, the dirty toes peeking through the holes in shoes. I am wearing boots; they're dusty. My new haircut makes me look younger. María, walking beside me, has a haircut that makes her look younger too. They are walking, we are all walking, as though in a parade—and it is all here: children crying and licking up the snot leaking from their noses, the maids dressed head-to-toe in black, the countrymen and countrywomen with their leathery, hard, somber, proud faces, the men in hats (also dry and leathery) to protect them from the sun, the local officials in their colorful T-shirts, their jeans, their rough cotton pants, their sparse moustaches that match their skin, their lean hands, their stiff, heavy, narrow-brimmed hats, the orchestra conductors, the official dressed in a long-tailed morning coat with a thick moustache (very well-trimmed and waxed), who had sung with the mariachis, a song by José Alfredo Jiménez that he sang as though it were an aria from an opera, the rich ladies that spend weekends in their luxurious country houses and play their grand pianos while Juan with a glass in his hand marks the beat, those ladies whose designer shoes are also getting dusty, walking along near the mariachis in their faded suits and their hoarse, boozy voices, beside the violinists and pianists who are not crying because men don't cry, beside the dwarf who's a flautist, the starving stray dogs with yellow eyes, the orchestra conductors in their dark gray pinstriped suits or fine cashmere navy blue blazers with gold buttons, the black cat that runs across the path (the ladies cross themselves) and the harpsichordist, who is actually grief-stricken, with red eyes and tears running down her cheeks (her eyes matching her dress, which is as elegant as María's, but of a differeeent cloth—brocade—and in a very different style, much less appropriate than María's for a funeral, although unquestionably very elegant; it's hard for her to walk on these pebbles, her heels are very high), the musicians from the orchestra (another black cat runs across the path, and the ladies cross themselves again), the orchestra that Juan conducted, all, or all the men, taking turns carrying the coffin, passing the casket from one to another, the coffin rocking and swaying on the shoulders of the men carrying it as they make their way along the path and lose their footing on the pebbles or slip on the cow dung and very softly spit out the word shit!—how else say shit at a funeral without the imprecation clashing with the perfectly cut navy blue blazers bought in New York or London? The thin blond woman who's with, or the companion of, the tall chestnut-haired woman has stepped in cow dung, too, and she, too, in a low but audible voice has, like the man in the Chicago-gangster pinstriped gray suit, pronounced the word shit!—they have both stepped in the cow dung, one after another, as they march along the rocky path, accompanying the body—maybe the same cow dung, the same cow shit plopped on the same place that all of them—the drunk and the thin well-dressed woman, the woman accompanying the other, taller woman with blond hair, both women dressed in white—have stepped in, and all of them, the drunk and the thin woman and the other woman, the one with the cloudy eye, at separate but successive instants, have stepped in the cow shit and have gotten it on them—the women, on their designer shoes, the beggar (his left foot stained with blood), on his tattered huaraches, the official wearing a navy blue blazer with gold buttons, on his well-polished black Church shoes covered with dust: he almost falls, he's just stepped in the same shit and softly spat out the same word: shit!

They come, we come, to the convent church, the procession enters the church, the coffin is placed near the altar, the shoulders and men rest, and the exequial mass begins, the funeral mass begins, the priest begins his sermon, a litany chanted in a mediocre, flat (though shrill) voice, and when the priest is done the mariachis begin singing; they have no range, they can't reach the high notes, the notes that sing of revenge, of courage, of machismo, they are third-rate Pedro Infantes, and their gestures, neither muted nor exaggerated by alcohol, translate their hard feelings. In the now weather-beaten and shedding wreaths one can read the town: near the church, a panel truck full of motorcycles; down in the street, the traffic policemen, the bowlegged, bribable motorcycle cops in their faded, ill-fitting dark-coffee or café con leche uniforms. At the four corners of the plaza, stalls selling carnitas, quesadillas, chorizos, delicate cigars, pan dulce, tortas, geese; the mourners entering the church one by one, others scattering in the atrium, some eating tacos in the plaza, while in the church the priest is chanting the funeral mass, a melancholy mass in the out-of-tune voice of the priest and the mariachis. Juan is in the coffin, surrounded by candles and covered with flowers, his body stiff, his face and clothes yellow, livid, the crucifix clutched to his chest (she was wearing a blue beret and a cross was hanging around her neck), his drab hay-colored moustache that covers a toothless mouth held firm by a black kerchief that binds his jaw tight. And through it all, like a litany, a rosary, a prayer, indifferent to the people singing, praying, murmuring their responses to the words of the priest, indifferent to those outside staggering around, shouting, accompanying the mariachis (singing endlessly), is the smell, a persistent, sickly-sweet smell, a dense smell of mold, of mildew. Some guy passes by me—is he one of those bureaucrats from the Treasury office, the Treasury office that will inventory the dead man's belongings, the pianos (how strange, I tell myself, I only saw the Bösendorfer, and the Steinway has disappeared! do you suppose Juan sold it? Schubert can only be performed on a Bösendorfer), the violins, the books, the scores, the CDs, the paintings, the chairs, the portraits, the pine chair I sat in, near the coffin, facing María; the china, the sheets, the towels, the pots and pans, the skillets, the four bottles of Zdhanov liquid? The things, in a word, all the things, always the things, the things that survive the dead. On the pew, near me, the beggar takes a seat—the beggar that stinks of alcohol and has one of his huarache-clad feet bandaged, the blood fresh and the bandage covered with dirt and cow shit—he is praying, too. You can hear someone sobbing, interrupting the priest's words, the singing of the mariachis, the conversations that some of the mourners are carrying on in lowered voices; people, curious, look around—it's a dark-skinned young man, not very tall, smooth hairless face, and he is crying unashamedly; his mother consoles him, he goes on crying; the beggar also looks at him with an expression of shock—what? aren't men not supposed to cry? And I observe him, turning around to do so (do you suppose it's him that one should give one's most heartfelt condolences to?) (do you suppose he's the only person who genuinely mourns his death?) (do you suppose I am?) (someone should give me their condolences, I think, I feel I need them, that I really do need them). I look at him impertinently, rudely almost, until a look from his mother puts me in my place. I lower my head, envelop myself in the smell again, the smell that is following me, that has followed me from the house to the church; the boy's crying had given me a moment's respite. All around, praying, other beggars, a few black-suited bureaucrats, their polyester shirts sweated through, women, children, countrypeople; the heat is dreadful, and the smells mingle with the fragrance of incense, and the sickly-sweet smell disappears for a few moments, mixing with the other smells. There are people carrying thick candles; beside the bureaucrat, a woman dressed in black, with glasses and boots; part of the pew is unoccupied and some men with uncombed hair slide into it: they've just come from the cantina; a stocky man in shirtsleeves, with a provocative look, I recognize him, he said hello to me at the house while he gave orders to people running around busily, putting lights in the trees while the cooks were cooking in a kind of tent, an awning on four legs, with charcoal stoves and big aluminum pots, the women that are there especially to cook and wait on the gentlemen, the pianists, the fertilizer salesmen, the traffic cops, the government officials wearing navy blue blazers, the elegant ladies, the town's Treasury agents, the bigots that have stayed up all night, the reporters, a cellist, the pianist, and the mayor.

Eduardo is a man so large, so corpulent that fatuousness in him would be a redundancy, and yet he is fatuous. He has installed himself alongside the tomb, displacing everyone else, his long white beard blowing in the wind; he takes up almost the entire right side of the grave and stands tall, majestic; he looks at me again, I am facing him, across the open grave, not too close, there is almost no one near me, the mourners have followed the procession to the little chapel in the cemetery; Eduardo gives me a little wave, his hands swollen by obesity and age, and to his eyes there comes a mocking smile (mocking what?, seeing me there, in front of him, shrunken?). The procession returns from the church, the body has taken its place twice before the altar, twice the body has been present, once at the mass in the main church, the second time in the cemetery chapel, and passionate, patriotic words have been spoken: the priest, a mayor, a fertilizer salesman, and a singer who modulates his voice as though it were the voice of a trumpet playing the Dies Irae, though never attaining the solemnity of Mozart's Requiem or of Juan's voice when he was telling us about the death of Bishop Fernández de Santa Cruz; that elegant, bearded singer that accompanied the mariachis, singing a song by José Alfredo Jiménez as though it were an aria from an opera, has also fallen silent. People begin to arrive, a swarm of women pushes to find a place next to the grave, four men bring the body, the priest blesses it, and the men from the mortuary take the coffin and begin lowering it, little by little, into the grave, the deep dark hole where the clay revolts; in their boozy voices the mariachis sing I tell you, crying in rage, the women and children sob, throw flowers—camellias, carnations, tuberoses, lilies (the fragrance of the lilies momentarily masks the constant smell of mold, of mildew) (I am riding the train of memory) (I remember Pergolesi again) (the flowers or the red roses) (I will not be back, I tell you, crying in rage, this is a one-way ticket, sing the mariachis) (the smell of mildew becomes stronger). Eduardo is still usurping the entire graveside—since when is he such a great friend of Juan's?, or has he decided to appear to be, to simply pretend to be, his best friend?, why wasn't he at the church?—do you suppose he's an atheist?, an atheist among the incense and crucifixes?—, why, then, wasn't he the principal speaker? I lower my head, a penetrating gaze makes me lift my eyes: it's Eduardo, spying on me. Is he moved by some perverse interest in seeing my reactions? His look is like the squirrel-that-looks-like-a-rat's.

People speak ill of others at a funeral; people gossip, and when the person they're talking about appears, they change expression—what expression do they have, what expression do they put on when I pass by and see them, when I hear bits and pieces of conversations (to prevent heart attacks, you should take an aspirin every morning, or better yet, 20 drops of garlic for ten days, diluted in tequila)? Conversations I stumble into and overhear, in which I suddenly hear my name (do you suppose they're speaking ill of me?), and the minute the people talking see me they turn their heads and pretend, change the subject (...I'll tell you, I'm telling you, they didn't get along at all, at all) (it was just the appearance) (: then he told her, why don't you go to the beach for a few days with the children?) (and when she came back she found the house empty, totally empty—he'd even taken the Persian carpets) (he was crazy, crazy, crazy!, and everybody knew it, a madman, though not a troublemaker) (his arteries were totally clogged) (he had almost no blood at the end; he was given three transfusions: he almost died three times) (the pain of a heart attack is as bad as the pain of childbirth) (to whom does one give one's most heartfelt condolences?) (some herbs help lower cholesterol: eryngo or a concentration of bald cypress). While they tell their endless, banal stories, María is eating her mouth; I am taken aback at the glaucous eye of the woman in red; I stare in fascination at the dusty huaraches and the bandaged left foot of the beggar, the drops of blood still fresh, Juan still lying in the coffin with that now-expressionless face: he is no longer among us, he is in the coffin made of rough pine, rough white pine with gold metal fittings, his toothless mouth unspeaking, especially now that his jaw has been bound with a black kerchief.

I feign, I make my face expressionless, I pretend I've heard nothing, I pretend I know no one. The truth is, many of the faces don't speak to me anymore, I've forgotten them: Eduardo, on the other hand, is impossible to forget; I hear his voice boom, he is surrounded by people, he is making grandiose gestures with his hands, his gigantic, wrinkled hands, and his fast-graying beard quivers. There is just one woman in that group, the small, thin woman without a drop of makeup on her face who is listening to him enthralled. A pause from Eduardo, the woman rushes in and in a stentorian voice exclaims: Only children and drunks tell the truth, and sometimes not even drunks (where did that contralto—castrato?—voice come from? a woman with such a tiny body!) (from her hoarse chest?). She looks at me out of the corner of her eye, purses her lips, a wrinkle makes her whole face quiver. I keep walking, I ignore her, I go from group to group, not paying much attention to what people are saying, although I do retain some conversations despite their insignificance, or perhaps because of it, because they're insignificant and that distracts me—no, repeats a short, red-faced, very dark-skinned man wearing very thick glasses and holding a pipe in his hand, one of whose fingers has a nail that is swollen, rough, deformed, grotesque—no, I tell you, he says, Joaquín will be the winner, I have a hunch about it.

I lower my head, I'm nauseated, the words follow me, hound me, haunt me, the smell envelops me, the smell that has followed, hounded, haunted me since the living room where the body was laid in state—it floated out to the street, from the street climbed up to the church, where the young man's weeping (weeping that came from the heart, weeping filled with the most profound grief) has given me a brief respite. Around me, praying, several people. The sickly-sweet odor disappears again for a few moments as it is swallowed up by the smell of the candles and the weeping of the dark-skinned young man, thick candles that some mourners are carrying; a woman dressed in dark gray, with glasses and low-heeled shoes, very sober and elegant, has approached and taken a seat on the same pew I'm on—it's María. The beggar has disappeared; on the pew behind me several men with uncombed hair have settled; they've just come from the cantina. I suddenly feel a heat, actually a prickling, itching (something's bitten me, I feel a prickling, itching all over my body—how embarrassing!), how strange, I think, and how ridiculous: scratching at a funeral; still, the itching gets worse and I discreetly scratch (what pleasure!). I mustn't forget that I'm in church, that this is a solemn occasion, that I am listening to a funeral mass, that there are many people: my body begins to be covered with welts, as though I'd lain naked on an anthill—a red fire-ant anthill—I itch everywhere, do you suppose it's mange?, the effect of the smell of mold, of mildew?, some terrible allergy to the people around me?, or a sophisticated manifestation of grief? Do you suppose that now they'll give me their most heartfelt condolences?

The procession is about to return, the body has lain before the altar twice, twice it has been present at the funeral mass, once at the mass in the main church, the second time in the cemetery chapel, impassioned, patriotic words of farewell have been spoken over it, words that come from the heart: the priest, the mayor, a fertilizer salesman, and a singer who modulates his voice like the voice of a trumpet playing the Dies Irae, although he does not attain the solemn percussion of Mozart's Requiem. People mill about, a swarm of women makes a place for itself beside the grave, but Eduardo is inflexible, unyielding, forceful, and he remains standing, prefiguring the monument whose statue will later, when a year has passed, eternalize a personage, a public figure, Juan. Four men carry the body, the priest blesses it, the men from the mortuary take it from them and begin to lower the casket, little by little, into the grave, women and children sob, throw flowers—camellias, carnations, tuberoses, lilies, crape myrtles, impatiens, gladiolas, camellias (the fragrance of the tuberoses briefly masks the constant smell of mold, of mildew) and finally a red rose falls—identical to the rose that the anonymous admirer of Pergolesi threw onto the stage of the Teatro di Argentina, in Rome, when the great composer was bemoaning his failure, shortly before he died of a heart broken to pieces.

In the church, while the funeral mass is being sung, I remember a French film from the early thirties, called Le Sang des Bêtes—there are huge men, hardened or immune to death and blood and stench, and they kill a white horse with an instrument that deals an instantaneous death-blow, and then they plunge a sharp knife into the beast's belly or its throat and black blood gushes out: it smokes and burns—they take out its steaming heart (the heart is just a muscle) (A man, goaded on by his lover, kills his pregnant wife by stabbing her seven times in the heart, and from her chest come just two or three drops of blood (Nastasya Filippovna?), then he takes his eight-year-old son and six-year-old daughter and slashes each of their throats with a kitchen knife and throws their bodies in the river: the blood gushes out). A repetitive, ritual, systematic movement gives meaning to, frames what I am watching in fascination, on the verge of nausea, in my house, sitting before the television or in the living room, looking at the body, listening to María or in the church while the mass is being sung, surrounded by government officials, musicians, bureaucrats, women, old men, children, and beggars, or beside the grave, standing across from Eduardo. It's a grayish, grainy documentary, a very old copy but you can see the blood perfectly clearly, thick blood, black, coagulating slowly in the copy being shown: an old, faded copy whose color resembles the suits of the mariachis who at this funeral I arrived at not long ago and at which I am standing, near the casket, are singing outdoors with their out-of-tune voices, and all the mourners have a glass of tequila in their hand, and they are chatting and smiling. The color of the mariachis' suits is as faded and dirty as the color of the documentary, and yet in the documentary you can clearly see the blood when it runs from the mutilated horse—it leaves a thick, viscous stain which spreads, throbs, the stain lengthening, coagulating in seconds: the horse and the man who has wounded it quivering, the blood spilling, running along the floor of the old Paris abattoir where, at this very instant I am watching it, they are killing the beast, plunging the knife into its throat or its belly or through its heart (which they take out, still hot—

open heart surgery is like butchery), then, when the horse is dead, they begin to cut it into pieces, and they cut its skin off with cleavers, hammers, saws, and they cut the bones one after another, separate the fat and the entrails little by little, you can see the heart clearly, it is smoking, steaming, and it is still beating (100 beats a minute!), and the body is quartered, little by little, and all that is left of the handsome white horse are shreds and tatters—tatters and shreds of meat and bone.

There is a need to explore the weave of marks and to combine, permute the signifying elements of the image, their function within the several homogeneous series established with respect to their origin, the nature of objects, the subjects figured there. I do not know the place occupied by certain animals (serpents, lizards, squirrels, birds, wild beasts, rats, cats, insects, cows, even roses), especially the horse in the imaginary that surrounds the figure of the Gorgon Medusa. In many representations, the horse—or horses placed symmetrically—is associated with her as though it could never be dissociated from that image and that trade—they are her prolongation or her emanation, like Perseus' horse Pegasus, the horse that appears the moment Perseus cuts off the Medusa's head. In these cases, in which the horse is associated with the Medusa, an excess and overflow of meaning occurs.

One of the most interesting museums in Boston is the Isabella Stewart Gardner—Gardner being a millionairess immortalized by John Singer Sargent, a painter detested by Mark Rothko because he painted only the powerful. In the portrait, Gardner is wearing a sober black silk dress with a modest neckline (the first curves of her bosom, very white, can be seen). The dress is very tight at her waist (she is wearing a corset) with a sort of belt formed of two strands of pearls, identical in size and drape to the choker about her throat—the finest pearls, clasped by a ruby set in gold. Her overskirt exaggerates her hips and thighs and creates a silhouette totally different from the anorexic models of today. Her hands are clasped before her, at the level of her loins, and they repeat the line of the pearl sash. Mrs. Gardner wears no makeup—at that time it would have been a flagrant sign of vulgarity (I recall a famous passage from Proust's novel in which a young woman of the upper class appears with just a bit of makeup in the street in Paris: the narrator's grandmother never speaks to the girl again). Behind her, as though it were a halo, a gold silk brocade covers the wall, and the painting becomes darker and darker toward the bottom until the black of the dress fades into the background, so that the spectator can only just make out a pair of satin shoes decorated with ruby brooches.

The Gardner Museum has furniture, tapestries, paintings, many of which were purchased on the advice of Bernard Berenson, the great expert in Italian painting and one of the first to reevaluate the masters of the early Renaissance. The museum, in fact, has two Mantegnas and several portraits of young patrician women painted by Uccello and Pollaiuolo; a Hercules by Piero della Francesca; a painting by Cosimo (or Cosmè) Tura, painter to the ducal d'Este family at the court of Ferrara, and another, with reminders of the Orient, by the Venetian painter Carlo Crivelli, those same painters that line the galleries dedicated to the Italian Quattrocento in the British Museum in London, painters spoken of by Edith Wharton in a lovely tale: it tells the story of a young New England heir whose taste runs to a delicate morbosity avant la lettre, a pallid aesthete who, on his obligatory trip to Italy, purchases paintings by artists of no value on the market (the same ones we are able to admire today in Isabella Stewart Gardner's museum), for which error in judgment his father disinherits him.

The museum is an old Venetian palazzo brought from Italy to New England, and it contains objects of the most dreadful taste cheek-by-jowl with marvels: draperies, Japanese screens, furniture, stained-glass windows, wonderful paintings, such as one, for example, by Sofonisba Anguissola, the Italian painter who lived at the court of Philip II of Spain and painted like Claudio Coello. The house is built around a loggia with a conservatory filled with orchids and lemon trees that produce enormous lemons, almost like gigantic grapefruit, rough-skinned and lustrous yellow, the green of the trees' leaves comparable only to the trees painted in the Renaissance—from the windows of the room in which the Virgin receives the angel of the annunciation one can look out on a landscape as unreal as the green of the leaves and the blue of the sky. Next to the lemon trees, wild (ferocious?) orchids, giant ferns, and mutilated statues.

I have seen in the Gardner a little exhibit dedicated to Cosimo Tura, some 12 paintings in small format. A very special exhibit, the guard says in response to a visitor who asks disappointedly why the show has so few paintings. Two of the paintings were especially remarkable: a small Virgin dressed in deep purple velvet (the color very much like the Emmanuelle Kahn suit that María is wearing), very sober, although a bit décolleté, and a baby Jesus with the face of an adult, half smiling, half reflective, sliding off her lap. Across from it, the most important painting in the little exhibit, a Pietà portraying the desolate Virgin sitting on a sepulcher (a beautifully carved stone sarcophagus) with the body of Christ in her lap, the Son still convulsed, reflecting the suffering of martyrdom; his parted lips, a deep brown, reveal very white teeth that contrast with his livid, or more precisely bluish, skin, which is the same hue as the Madonna's mantle, whose thick, hard, sculptural folds fall to the ground, framing the body of Christ. The Virgin is wearing a black dress that reveals part of her throat; her head (in three-quarter profile) is covered with a gauze headdress that totally hides her hair: she brings her son's arm to her face as though she were going to kiss it (with an expression of profound melancholy). She is the same age as Christ, who, naked, his loins covered by a piece of cloth similar to his mother's headdress, has placed his left hand on his navel—one can see the wound made by the nail, drops of blood still fresh, very red, repeat the wound in his side, which is also bleeding: the face is Eastern, grotesque, reflecting an agony made all the more horrible by the narrow crown of thorns from which drip two streams of crystalline blood. Behind the figures, a strange landscape, Golgotha, a spiral mountain that rises and twists like the Tower of Babel; on top of it, three crosses—on two, the twisted bodies of the thieves, but the central cross is empty.

Tura's figures, Berenson says, seem sculpted of stone; they are as hieratic and immobile as the statues of the Egyptian pharaohs, but their convulsed yet contained energy reminds us of the knots that contort the thin trunks of olive trees. Tura is different from his contemporaries, the Florentine Sandro Botticelli for instance, whose idea of beauty is a delicate, classical simplicity.

I keep watching the documentary for a week (almost) after the funeral. One of the butchers is fierce and fat, with an archaic, dark face (the squirrel looks at me from the window, its eyes have softened, they no longer look like the eyes of a rat). Suddenly the butcher's cleaver misses its mark, and instead of striking the body of the horse he hits his own leg, and blood flows once more—steaming, black—and everything ends, the screen goes dark, and for just an instant, a bare instant afterward, so quickly one can barely catch the image, the camera shows the man with one good leg and one wooden one—he's not a butcher anymore, I say to myself, he's a pirate—, it's the left leg that's been cut off with the cleaver, and now it's a stub mounted on an archaic prosthesis; the cleaver, the same cleaver, moves skillfully, artfully, still dismembering, murdering the horses in the abattoir, in that old French abattoir located in a suburb of Paris, a Paris dark and dreary and low-class, before the Second World War, a Paris resembling those we see in the photographs by Brassaï and this documentary I am now looking at, or that now, beside the coffin, looking at him, at Juan, listening to María and seeing her disappearing mouth, her mutilated face, her lips pursed in anger and resentment, I remember; I remember the dismembered bodies of horses piled up, higher and higher, more and more dismembered bodies of horses—I cannot bear the stench any longer, horror and nausea wash over me from the screen. I keep looking at the body lying before me, and I am possessed by the sickly-sweet smell, it encircles me like a halo—it will not leave me, will not leave him—at this very instant on the screen appear several gruff, muscular men, walking toward the enormous room in which the mutilated butcher is wielding his cleaver and little by little, one by one, they begin to put the pieces of the dismembered bodies on wide flat carts, which they will push out to fill the vans that will distribute the horse meat to the butcher shops that sell it: life is an absurd wound. Horse meat does not have the same flavor as beef; it is sweeter-tasting, and its sweetness is repugnant. I keep dreaming that I am lost: when I wake up I can never find myself, I suffer, it infuriates me, my heart beats fast.

In Georgia, in a crematory where the dead were supposed to be cremated, bodies were found in various states of decomposition. The families of the dead persons had received urns filled with dirt and cement dust.

I am standing before the coffin, I feel the blood circulate through my body, I feel my entrails, his entrails, writhing, churning, and with my heart already wounded by misfortune I recall the blood that falls into the horse's eyes, or the blood that runs down the butcher's leg, when, surprised by the pain, he sees the cleaver in his hand, the cleaver that has missed its mark and accidentally—accidentally?—mutilated him, as though he, he too, were a horse. I smell the blood again, the pure blood, and then the bile, the pure bile, the dry anger and resentment, the contained rage, the hatred that turns against me as though I stank and my violence were a contagion that spreads, attacks, threatens to overflow my skin, to let the blood pour out, gush out, the blood the cleaver has made gush out of that cut leg, the blood that drains toward the floor and accompanies the leg that falls and the face that watches it, the eyes bulging out of their sockets, the man still holding the cleaver in his hand—hot, viscous, dirty—his eyes fixed on his own blood, the blood that flows from the heart when the heart has been broken (they have replaced the mitral valve with a valve made of animal tissue) (it's a pig's or cow's) or when they have opened the chest cavity (an open heart operation), the heart shattered in my hands (they have replaced the damaged arteries with grafts, they have used the delicate arteries from the mammary glands) (or a bridge has been made with the saphenous artery), the blood mixed with the blood of the horse that leaves a mark on the stained floor of the slaughterhouse, and a sickly-sweet smell fills the screen, like that sickly-sweet smell that follows me and that cannot be masked even by the fragrance of the flowers (especially the tuberoses); neither the roses, even when they're red roses, nor the four open bottles of disinfectant (Zhdanov liquid) can mask the odor of corruption given off by the decomposed body of Nastasya Filippovna (Rogozhin has thought about surrounding Nastasya's body with roses, but he doesn't, it horrifies him that someone might (even) imagine that she is dead). That sickly-sweet odor does not disappear with the fragrance of the flowers or the smell or color of the candles: four, yes, set at the four corners of the casket.

I am alone, sitting before the screen, hypnotized, watching the documentary over and over, smelling the blood that spills despite the fact that there really is no blood in this yellow body that we are sitting beside. It is a lifeless, bloodless body.

Bloodless?, I wonder. The word bloodless, spoken like that, aloud, or whispered, reminds me immediately of a body in which the blood has stopped flowing, a body that truly has no blood. Life is an absurd wound: I believe I deserve to be given their most heartfelt condolences. It's obvious: in a living body the blood circulates constantly (the myocardium weighs between 250 and 300 grams, 50 to 100 beats a minute, a hundred thousand times a day) (Glenn Gould performed his last recording of the Goldberg Variations in 51 minutes, 15 seconds, in 1981) and this body, Juan's body, is no longer alive, it is dead, not a single beat from his heart, which simply means, I repeat infinitely in a low voice (though I do not understand), which simply means that the blood is no longer flowing, no longer circulating through his veins, his heart has stopped beating (50 to 100 beats a minute), the blood, I repeat, the blood, the blood cannot circulate when a body dies and when that muscle we know as the heart has begun to undergo necrosis.

The heart has reasons that reason knows nothing of, Pascal said.

I dreamed that I was getting lost. I awoke furious: I haven't found myself (my blood pressure shot up).

The body I sit beside in the large living room of the country house, where I am accompanied by a dense, perpetual smell of candles, tuberoses, and mold, mildew, has been placed in a casket made of unfinished white pine with metal fittings, and it is dressed in an olive-green suit and a banal tie; it has a crucifix clasped against its breast, its face is livid and slack-jawed, its eyes are sunken, its mouth is violet-colored, toothless, and above it there is a sparse, faded moustache; its lower jaw is tied with a black kerchief to hold it closed; the beautiful hands, the long, elegant fingers— yellow. This body, I conclude, no longer has any blood.

It is a bloodless, lifeless body.

A bloodless, lifeless body.

Coyoacán, Princeton, Coyoacán,
Harvard, Coyoacán
1999, 2001-2002

One of the most prolific and respected authors of Mexico, Margo Glantz is not only a distinguished award-winning novelist, but also acclaimed as a lecturer, critic, journalist, and translator. She teaches literature at the National University of Mexico, and she has been resident writer and scholar at various universities in the United States, including Yale, Harvard, and Princeton.

CURBSTONE PRESS, INC.

is a non-profit publishing house dedicated to literature that reflects a commitment to social change, with an emphasis on contemporary writing from Latino, Latin American and Vietnamese cultures. Curbstone presents writers who give voice to the unheard in a language that goes beyond denunciation to celebrate, honor and teach. Curbstone builds bridges between its writers and the public – from inner-city to rural areas, colleges to community centers, children to adults. Curbstone seeks out the highest aesthetic expression of the dedication to human rights and intercultural understanding: poetry, testimonies, novels, stories, and children's books.

This mission requires more than just producing books. It requires ensuring that as many people as possible learn about these books and read them. To achieve this, a large portion of Curbstone's schedule is dedicated to arranging tours and programs for its authors, working with public school and university teachers to enrich curricula, reaching out to underserved audiences by donating books and conducting readings and community programs, and promoting discussion in the media. It is only through these combined efforts that literature can truly make a difference.

Curbstone Press, like all non-profit presses, depends on the support of individuals, foundations, and government agencies to bring you, the reader, works of literary merit and social significance which might not find a place in profit-driven publishing channels, and to bring the authors and their books into communities across the country. Our sincere thanks to the many individuals, foundations, and government agencies who have recently supported this endeavor: Community Foundation of Northeast Connecticut, Connecticut Commission on Culture & Tourism, Connecticut Humanities Council, Greater Hartford Arts Council, Hartford Courant Foundation, Lannan Foundation, National Endowment for the Arts, and the United Way of the Capital Area.

Please help to support Curbstone's efforts to present the diverse voices and views that make our culture richer. Tax-deductible donations can be made by check or credit card to:
Curbstone Press, 321 Jackson Street, Willimantic, CT 06226
phone: (860) 423-5110   fax: (860) 423-9242
www.curbstone.org

IF YOU WOULD LIKE TO BE A MAJOR SPONSOR OF A
CURBSTONE BOOK, PLEASE CONTACT US.